Moistening her lips, she brought a trembling hand to her chest.

For a quick, hot second, he thought she might let the towel drop. He pictured her untwisting the terrycloth and standing naked before him, offering herself. In the next heartbeat, he'd have her legs around his waist and her back against the wall.

But she didn't loosen her towel; she clutched it tight. "I can't."

That made two of them. "Why not?"

Her throat worked as she swallowed. "It's complicated."

His raging hormones disagreed. They said it was as easy as unbuttoning his trousers and urging her down on his lap.

"I like you—"

"I like you, too."

Her eyes filled with anguish. "You don't even know me."

"Then let me get to know you," he said, frustrated. "Why won't you tell me what those men want? What have you done that's so bad?"

She let her shoulders rest on the wall behind her, staring up at the ceiling. "They think I killed someone."

"Did you?"

Her gaze reconnected

Dear Reader,

Thanks so much for picking up my latest Harlequin Romantic Suspense novel. I had a blast writing this one and hope you enjoy reading it.

Before we got married, my husband and I went on a three-week trip through central Mexico, visiting archaeological sites, colonial towns and coastal cities. We had such a great time that we returned two years later to tour the Yucatan Peninsula. Being from San Diego, we've also crossed the border for many weekend excursions to Baja California. I love the warmth and vibrancy of Latin America. *Viva Mexico!*

With *Tempted by His Target,* I wanted to give readers a fun, exciting vacation in a foreign country. My heroine, Isabel Sanborn, is one hot target. She's on the run and in need of protection when she teams up with the hero, Brandon North. This is a high-octane romance, so get ready for car chases, close proximity and sizzling sexual tension.

Enjoy!

Jill Sorenson

JILL SORENSON

Tempted by His Target

ROMANTIC

SUSPENSE

PROM
Sorenson

Recycling programs
for this product may
not exist in your area.

ISBN-13: 978-0-373-27748-3

TEMPTED BY HIS TARGET

www.Harlequin.com

Printed in U.S.A.

Books by Jill Sorenson

Harlequin Romantic Suspense
Stranded With Her Ex #1654
Tempted by His Target #1678

Silhouette Romantic Suspense
Dangerous to Touch #1518

JILL SORENSON

writes sexy romantic suspense for Harlequin Books and Bantam. Her books have appeared in *Cosmopolitan* magazine.

After earning a degree in literature and a bilingual teaching credential from California State University, she decided teaching wasn't her cup of tea. She started writing one day while her firstborn was taking a nap and hasn't stopped since. She lives in San Diego with her husband and two young daughters.

To Chris, my favorite traveling companion.

Chapter 1

Brandon stood at the edge of the beach, where jungle met sand, and watched his quarry wade out of the ocean.

He hadn't expected to find her this soon.

Izzy Sanborn, aka Isabel Sanchez, dropped her surf-board on the shore, sluicing water from her dark hair. Her bikini top was snug, clinging to her lithe upper body, but her boardshorts were too large, almost falling off her hips. She knelt down on the sand, her back to him, and inspected what appeared to be a broken fin.

His heart began to pound with anticipation. Puerto Escondido was famous for big waves, and he was almost as eager to paddle out as he was to get his woman. Oaxaca's "Mexican Pipeline" rivaled the strength and size of Oahu's North Shore. Surfers from all over the world came here to test their mettle.

Ms. Sanborn had quite a bit of mettle, apparently. The beach was deserted and the conditions were precarious.

Surfing here with no protective equipment was dangerous. Doing it alone was damned near suicidal.

Brandon strode forward, aware that she couldn't hear him approach over the crashing waves. He hadn't planned to sneak up on her but he knew that she avoided strangers. She might bolt if she saw him coming.

Before he had a chance to announce his presence, she tilted her head, catching sight of him out of the corner of her eye. Quick as a cat, she leaped over her surfboard, drawing up the leg of her shorts. There was a dagger strapped to her upper thigh.

He was impressed by her quick reflexes, and more than a little concerned that she would try to gut him like a fish. Resisting the urge to drop into a protective stance, he waited for her to make a move. Instead of unsheathing her weapon and launching an unprovoked attack, she slipped her hand out from under the hem of her shorts and straightened. She also relaxed her face, as if nothing was amiss.

"I'm sorry," he said, keeping a cautious distance between them. "I didn't mean to scare you."

She remained silent, her expression cool now, impossible to read. Without being too obvious about it, he studied her appearance. Her black knit bikini top molded to her breasts in a tempting way. She had a trim figure: flat belly, slim waist, curvy hips. Every inch of her was smooth and tanned and toned. Strong, but decidedly feminine.

He lifted his gaze to her face, noting that she was even prettier in person. Her features were well arranged, her mouth nicely shaped. With her thick, dark lashes and fine brown eyes, she was striking.

Brandon had seen her picture in magazines, and memorized every detail, so he shouldn't have been caught off guard by her beauty. He shouldn't have been dazzled by it, either. For some reason, she made him feel like an awkward teen again. The circumstances were unusual, of course. He'd never had a female target before.

To put her at ease, he repeated his apology in awkward Spanish, as if he wasn't sure she'd understood him.

She crossed her arms over her chest, more annoyed now than wary. "I speak English."

"Cool," he said, flashing a friendly smile. "You're a really good surfer. Those were some sick moves."

"Thanks."

"Too bad about the broken fin."

She shrugged. "It happens."

"This looks like a tricky break. And a sharp reef."

"Yes. Not for amateurs."

"You surf alone?"

"All the time."

"Wow," he said, shaking his head. "You have more co-jones than I do."

He'd meant that figuratively, but her gaze drifted down to the Velcro fly of his boardshorts, as if checking out his male anatomy. His stomach muscles tightened on reflex and she glanced away, flushing.

Brandon watched a bead of salt water travel down the side of her face, fascinated. Her complexion wasn't so dusky that he couldn't see a tinge of pink on her cheeks. He wondered if she was embarrassed by his offhand remark, or angry with him for invading her privacy. "Can you give me some pointers?"

"You've got no business here if you're inexperienced."

"I'm experienced enough," he said mildly.

"What do you see out there?"

He did a quick assessment. "This is a high-tide break. At low, the reef will be exposed, and the wave probably closes out. Swells are far-spaced, height is overhead and there's a slight onshore flow."

"Very slight."

Brandon nodded with real pleasure. The only thing better was no wind at all. "Does it get any glassier than this?"

"Not much," she admitted.

He moistened his lips, hungry for a taste of those waves. Intrigued by his most challenging assignment to date. "Will you spot me?"

It was clear that she wanted to say no, but surfing etiquette required her to agree. Refusing a safety request was like dropping in on another man's wave, or trying to steal his girl. It just wasn't done. "Okay," she said, sighing. "I'll keep an eye on you for thirty minutes. Maybe you can catch a few."

Grinning, he offered her his hand. "I'm Brandon North, by the way."

She smiled back, seeming amused by his enthusiasm, and her beauty took his breath away. In the years since her last photo shoot, she'd lost softness in her cheeks and dropped the exaggerated pout. Maturity suited her. She was confident, mysterious…and twice as appealing. "Isabel," she said, accepting his handshake.

"Isabel," he repeated. "Can I buy you lunch after this?"

She jerked her hand out of his. "No."

"Do you eat alone, too?"

Her smile disappeared and she sat down on the sand, ignoring his question. "The reef is brutal," she warned, dusting off her knees. "You're better off taking a dive than risking a wipeout."

Avoiding risk wasn't his style, but he didn't say that.

"The wave moves fast once it hollows," she continued.

"If you get a chance to stay inside the curl, go for it. It's a luscious barrel."

He eyed the formation, experiencing a rush of adrenaline that wasn't unlike arousal. Sometimes he'd rather surf than have sex. Lately he hadn't done enough of either.

Aware that Isabel was watching him, he pulled his attention from the water. Despite her dark coloring, she didn't look like a native. Her skin was honey-gold, sun-warmed rather than God-given. Beneath her bikini top, she would be pale and delicate. He imagined pushing the wet fabric aside, revealing her bare breasts and soft nipples.

What Brandon felt now wasn't similar to arousal; it *was* arousal. His face went taut as he struggled to stay cool. She stared back at him, her gaze burning into his, and a spark ignited inside him. He had the feeling that she knew exactly what he was thinking.

Her eyes trailed down his stomach again, lingering at the waistband of his shorts, which were riding low on his hips. "Go on," she said, refocusing on the waves. It was both a dismissal and a challenge.

Muttering his thanks, he strode toward the shore. The sand beneath his bare feet was a pearly gray, darkened by volcanic ash and littered with crushed shells. Not pristine, but still very beautiful. The water was so clear he could make out the sharp-toothed reef beneath the surface, and the waves broke hard against it, creating one of the sleekest curls he'd ever seen.

His pulse thundered in his ears. He'd been surfing for more than ten years—that was the reason he'd been chosen for this assignment—but he wasn't used to waves like this. The height was intimidating. It also reminded him that he was here to gain Isabel's trust as a dedicated athlete, not to picture her naked.

Brandon waded into the foam-specked surf, determined to impress her. The water was only a few degrees cooler than the balmy air. He felt immersed in pleasure as it enveloped him. In San Diego, the ocean was so cold he usually needed a wet suit, but like most surfers, he preferred to trunk it.

He tossed his board on the water and leaped on top of it, paddling with easy, practiced motions. Ducking under the first wave, he resurfaced on the other side and kept moving to a calmer area beyond the breakers.

When he was in the right position, he turned back toward the beach, straddling his board and sitting upright.

Isabel was watching, waiting.

A decent six came up fast. Lying down again, he headed for the rising swell and paddled hard, standing up just as it gained momentum. His footing was off by a fraction. He lost his balance and the board went flying, propelled by the force of the wave.

Managing to avoid the reef, even while the whitewash swirled like a vortex around him, he felt the tug of his leash and followed it back to the surface. After securing his board carefully, because he'd been hit in the face by a rogue surfboard too many times to count, he cast another glance at the beach. Isabel looked bored.

He redoubled his efforts. His next few tries were more successful, and he fell into a nice rhythm. Although he didn't forget his audience, he started surfing for himself. Ten minutes after he paddled out, a set of high overheads rolled in behind him. They rose up from the sea like liquid monoliths, ten thousand gallons of pure power.

He positioned himself at the top of the swell and let it take him. The wave moved so fast he hardly had to paddle. Holding steady, he popped up, bracing his feet on the surface of the board and lifting his arms.

A split second later, he cut to the right, and the curl folded over him in a perfect hollow. The feeling was so exhilarating he let out a triumphant shout as he maneuvered through the tube, fighting to stay inside.

Now this——*this* was how it felt to be alive. Here, he was in his element, with a powerful wave all around him, a killer reef beneath the surface and a sexy woman waiting for him on a deserted beach.

The ride wasn't his all-time best, but it was pretty damned good. In the top ten, for sure. He executed a serviceable cutback and sank into the whitewash as the hollow closed out, narrowly avoiding a run-in with the razor-edged reef.

When he broke through the surface, he steadied his board and wiped the water off his face, laughing out loud from the rush.

Isabel was gone.

His smile faded as he searched the edges of the mangrove for a glimpse of her retreating form. There was only a trail of small footprints heading into the jungle. She'd ditched him as soon as he got distracted. It was bad form, but not necessarily suspicious. He was a strange man; she had cause to be wary.

Instead of running after her, he waded out of the water and followed at a steady pace. This particular beach was only accessible by boat or via a twisty footpath. If Isabel's Jeep hadn't been parked by the side of the road, surf rack half-hidden by foliage, he'd never have found the entrance.

And if she hadn't written an "anonymous" article about this little-known spot for a popular surfing magazine, he'd never have found *her*.

Brandon still didn't know where she lived, but he knew what she drove, and Puerto Escondido wasn't a big city. He could probably locate her residence in short order. He could also tie her up and throw her in his trunk, if he had to. But strong-arm tactics were a last resort, and he wasn't supposed to make a scene.

He didn't want to alert the Mexican authorities—under any circumstances.

So he hitched his surfboard under one arm and navigated his way through the tangle of vines beyond the beach. The jungle appeared impenetrable. There were a few machete marks on the thick palm fronds, forming a barely discernible path. He could smell decomposing vegetation and recent rain. Life and death, blended.

Birdcalls echoed through the pungent depths. A buzzing sound started, growing louder in his ear. He slapped the mosquito on his neck, killing the noise.

After a summer in breezy San Diego, the humidity took some getting used to. The instant the salt water on his skin evaporated, beads of sweat formed on his chest. The jungle seemed to suck up every breath of air and inch of space. It was dark, too. When his eyes adjusted, he could no longer see footsteps on the ground, only hacked-up edges of plants and fallen leaves.

His surfboard shifted, growing slippery against his armpit.

He reached the edge of the clearing in time to watch Isabel's Jeep fly down the road, leaving him in the dust. Squinting at the sudden brightness, he stared after her, his blood pumping with adrenaline.

She was faster than he'd expected. Stronger, more resourceful. He was going to enjoy catching her.

Chapter 2

Isabel didn't lift her foot off the gas until she was five miles away.

She flexed her fingers around the steering wheel and glanced in the rearview mirror once again, her heart racing.

There was nothing behind her but dust.

Brandon had parked his rental vehicle, a midsize SUV, behind her Jeep. If he wanted to, he could follow her.

But why would he want to?

She took a deep breath, trying to relax. She'd run through the jungle like a maniac, half-convinced he was chasing her. Maybe she was overreacting, but his unexpected arrival had shaken her to the core. Leaving her back to the beach had been careless. She usually looked over her shoulder everywhere she went.

How could she have let him sneak up on her?

Muttering curses, she traveled south on the main highway for another mile before she pulled over, parking her Jeep behind a copse of trees. There she waited, monitoring the light flow of traffic as the sun crept high in the sky.

Brandon's silver SUV passed by less than fifteen minutes later, his shortboard sticking out of the back like a white flag.

She'd known at a glance that he didn't belong here. It took an experienced surfer to handle that break, but he wasn't a pro. He didn't travel with an entourage of photographers. His board was a rental. Big shots brought their own gear.

He wasn't a burnout, either. Puerto Escondido attracted its share of scraggly potheads who were more interested in getting blazed than honing their surfing skills. Brandon didn't fit that mold at all. With his close-cropped hair, clean-shaven jaw and sharp blue eyes, he looked like a straight arrow.

He was also hot as hell. His features were rugged and masculine, his physique taut. Something about him suggested wealth or privilege. He was wearing light gray boardshorts and nothing else. He had muscles like an endurance athlete, not a heavy weight lifter. She could have stared at his chest all day.

Her first reaction to him had been panic. She'd registered his height and broad shoulders and assumed he was one of Carranza's men, come to kill her. Realizing that he wasn't Mexican didn't ease her anxiety. It wouldn't have surprised her if the drug lord had recruited an assassin from outside the cartel. But Brandon had wasted the perfect opportunity to take her out, and he didn't look like a thug.

Maybe she should have had lunch with him.

Shaking her head, Isabel started the engine and pulled out of her hiding place, following his SUV back to town.

It wasn't smart to get distracted by a killer body and a handsome face. Over the past few days, she'd felt uneasy, as if someone was watching her. Perhaps Brandon was the culprit.

He stopped at The Pelican, a nice hotel within walking distance of the most popular beach in Puerto Escondido. Isabel made a left on the nearest cross street and circled around, catching a glimpse of him entering the hotel courtyard.

She continued driving, hoping he would stay in his room for a while. Her apartment was downtown, less than two miles away. She parked in the covered garage and hurried toward the wooden steps, glancing around for strangers. Everything looked normal. Street vendors were selling tacos to the lunchtime crowd. The smell of grilled fish, fresh-cut limes and chopped cilantro wafted up, making her mouth water.

After a quick shower, she changed into one of her casual outfits, loose-fitting cargo pants and a plain white shirt. She put her knife holster around her waist. Covering her eyes with sunglasses and her dark hair with a baseball cap, she left the apartment.

Isabel spoke Spanish fluently, thanks to her Venezuelan mother, but she didn't sound local, and she couldn't disguise her femininity. Instead of trying to pass for a man, or a native, she stayed quiet and wore nondescript clothing. This tactic, along with moving around a lot, had kept her alive the past two years.

But she'd grown weary of running. Puerto Escondido had a low-key atmosphere and fantastic surf conditions. She didn't want to leave.

Isabel bypassed the taco stand outside her apartment, her stomach growling. She usually had her groceries delivered and ate in. On rare occasions, she grabbed a quick bite on the other side of town. This stand was too close for comfort.

Climbing into her Jeep, she returned to the neighborhood by The Pelican, parking nearby. She'd never done surveillance before, but she'd read up on the subject. Approaching it from the watcher's perspective was a novel experience.

She chose an outdoor café with a good view of the hotel, sitting down with an iced coffee and a shrimp sandwich. After polishing off her meal, she helped herself to a newspaper, pretending to read. Brandon reappeared a short time later. He left his hotel and strolled east, toward the cluster of restaurants. She watched him from behind the newspaper, praying he wouldn't choose the café.

Again, she was struck by how attractive he was. He appeared relaxed and slightly rumpled in lightweight trousers and a short-sleeved shirt. Although he was obviously a tourist, he had a low-key vibe. His clothes fit well, accentuating a rock-hard physique. Scuffed hiking boots suggested he was an all-around outdoorsman, not just a beach bum. His short hair glinted like bronze in the sunlight. Her fingers itched to test its thickness.

She twisted her hands in the newspaper as he passed by.

Isabel wasn't the only woman in the vicinity who was aware of his presence. Two European girls in tank tops and gypsy skirts came out of a souvenir shop to gawk. They were pretty, if you liked braless bohemian babes. Brandon apparently did. He smiled at them, saying something that made one of the girls laugh and clutch her beaded hemp necklace.

A stab of envy pricked Isabel's heart. She hadn't flirted with a man, or dressed to impress, since she'd left California. In her former life, she'd worn flashy miniskirts and spike-heeled Louboutins. She didn't miss the expensive clothes, her swanky Hollywood Hills apartment, or even the rebellious rich boys she used to date, but she missed *people*. She missed friends, and familiar faces, and companionship.

Brandon didn't linger with the girls, to Isabel's surprise. They watched him go, giggling together before wandering back toward the beach.

Isabel frowned behind the newspaper. He'd invited her to lunch, but ignored two sexy young ladies on the prowl? That didn't add up right. Maybe she'd misinterpreted the situation. She folded her paper and put it back in the rack, tossing some coins on the table before she left the café.

He made another unexpected choice in selecting a place to eat. There were several palapa-style restaurants in the area, but they were all more expensive than the simple taco stands downtown. Instead of wandering into a touristy bar and grill, he walked east a few blocks, locating a busy street vendor.

Isabel stayed out of sight, pretending to shop for jewelry and handcrafts while Brandon put away more tacos than she could count. When he was finished, he thanked the vendor and headed back to the main drag. There were a couple of sports shops near the beach, including Smokey's, which rented surfboards.

Brandon stopped at EcoTours, the store next to Smokey's. It was closed, so he perused the sign in the front window. The business offered outrageously expensive tours to remote locations of Oaxaca, including the "secret" beach they'd just visited. Some surfers would pay anything for a chance to ride a virgin wave.

Brandon took his cell phone out of his pocket, dialing the number on the sign.

Isabel let out a frustrated sigh. She could show him

the least-crowded spots around here for a fraction of the price. He'd found Playa Perdida on his own, probably by noticing her vehicle parked at the side of the road.

If he wasn't American, and a possible threat, she might have approached him as a guide. She could use the money. But she couldn't take a chance on him recognizing her as Izzy Sanborn. The way he'd looked at her, as though he was picturing her naked, had made her squirm with a pleasant sort of discomfort. He was in his late twenties, at the most, and her photo spreads had been very popular with young men.

He moved on, ducking into the least authentic place in all of Puerto Escondido: Señor Frog's Cantina. The bar catered to loudmouthed college students and hosted wet T-shirt contests. It was a puke party every night.

"Ugh," she said, disappointed by his bad taste. She couldn't follow him in, so she took a small notebook and a pen out of her satchel. Propping her back against a brick wall on the opposite side of the street, she got some work done, scribbling notes about this morning's session at Playa Perdida. In the past few months, she'd sold several articles to *Wave* magazine, written anonymously as the Lost Surfer.

The paycheck was small, but she'd been delighted to receive it. She had a fake ID as Isabel Sanchez and a PO Box set up here in Puerto Escondido. When the check came, her heart had swelled with pride.

It was the first time she'd earned money with her *brain*.

An hour later, Brandon came out of Señor Frog's, and she'd outlined a new article. He must have knocked back a few drinks, because he had the loose-hipped gait of a man who was feeling his spirits. Isabel put her notebook away, relieved. He was just another party animal surf jock. A paid assassin would be more circumspect.

She followed him back to the hotel anyway, not worrying overmuch about being seen. He took a wrong turn, wandering down a cobblestone alley. This late in the afternoon, the area was quiet, dim and deserted.

Isabel removed her sunglasses and put them in her pocket, annoyed by his recklessness. Not only was he drunk and alone in a foreign country, he was begging to get mugged. He might as well leave his wallet on the beach while he went for a swim.

He disappeared around the corner and she hurried after him, sticking close to the back of the building. She paused at the edge, listening for footsteps. Her hand wavered by her knife, fingertips tingling. She heard nothing.

Afraid of losing him, she stepped out of the alleyway. A flash of movement startled her into action. She leaped backward, drawing her knife. Brandon caught her wrist in a crushing grip and spun her around, shoving her against the wall.

Gasping in pain, she dropped her weapon. When he eased his hold on her wrist, she wrenched her arm from his grasp and slammed her left elbow into his midsection. Whirling to face him, she aimed a hard right at his throat.

He blocked it easily. Too easily.

Isabel realized a couple of things at once. First, he wasn't drunk. Second, he knew how to fight. Third, he was surprised to see her.

"You," he breathed, backing up a step and holding a palm to his midsection. "I thought somebody was trying to rob me."

She flattened her back against the wall, her heart thumping in her chest. She'd mistaken his level of inebriation and made a serious error in judgment. Her knife glinted on the cobblestones, out of reach.

He followed her gaze, his eyes narrowing. "*Are* you trying to rob me?"

"No," she said, moistening her lips.

"I have ten dollars in my wallet. Do you want it?"

"No! I saw you come out of the cantina and I was trying to catch up with you."

"Why?"

She swallowed hard. "I'd like to offer my services as a tour guide. I know all of the best surf spots."

He crossed his arms over his chest, deliberating. "How much?"

"Fifty a day, U.S."

"What does that include?"

She thought fast. "I'll take you to a choice location, spot you for a few hours of surfing and bring lunch."

"You'll drive?"

"Sure. My Jeep has a surf rack."

"Okay," he said, nodding. It was a much better deal than he'd get from EcoTours. They made arrangements for her to pick him up at his hotel in the morning, and shook hands. Isabel felt the same zing of pleasure as she had the first time he'd touched her.

He released her hand slowly, a crease forming between his brows. "I don't pay women for sex."

She recoiled in horror. "Of course not."

"I just wanted to make sure that wasn't on the table," he said, raising both palms. "Don't attack me again."

Her cheeks warmed with embarrassment. "Sorry about that. Gut reaction."

He studied her for a moment, as if wondering who or what had made her so cautious. Instead of asking, he minded his own business. "Can I walk you home?"

"No thanks. I have another stop to make."

"See you tomorrow then."

"Tomorrow."

She reached down to retrieve her knife, watching him walk away. When he was out of sight, she sheathed the blade, hurrying down the alley. As she rounded the corner, she almost collided with a stocky man in a fedora.

There was an odd moment, not unlike the one she'd just had with Brandon, in which Isabel experienced a jolt of awareness. She looked into this man's cold, dark eyes and knew: it wasn't Brandon who'd been following her.

Before she could react to that certainty, the stranger reached out to grab her upper arm. He also flipped back the tails of his shirt, revealing a handgun tucked in his waistband. He was in his fifties, about Carranza's age, but hardly soft. "Come with me," he said in a low voice, his lips curled into a tight grimace.

Isabel was already primed for action, and she'd trained for this occasion. She lashed out, striking his forearm in a brutal chop. His grip loosened, but he backhanded her across the face, trying to subdue her.

The tactic worked. Pain exploded in her left cheek, hot and bright. Knocked off balance, she spun around and almost fell to her knees. When he grabbed her by the hair, she cried out, certain he was going to execute her. Panicking, she drew her knife and stabbed backward, using the same motion as an elbow jab.

The blade found its target, sliding to the hilt in a sickening plunge. Blood spurted over her hand and the man let out a hoarse cry, releasing her hair. She lunged forward, taking the knife with her, and turned to evaluate the damage.

"*Puta*," he spat, holding his side. As blood seeped between his fingers, shock blanched his weathered countenance.

Isabel's heart dropped. The wound appeared life-threatening.

Using his other hand, the man reached for his gun. She could only stare, her mind blank with terror as he leveled the barrel at her.

Chapter 3

Brandon knew Isabel had been following him. He'd caught a glimpse of her at the café, and another after he left the bar.

As soon as they parted ways, he doubled back, returning the favor.

He doubted she really wanted to be his surf guide, although that was the outcome he'd been fishing for. His mission was to get her out of the country without using brute force. Tomorrow he planned to drop a few hints about continuing the tour in Guatemala and hope she took the bait. Very few surfers visited that section of the Pacific Coast. It was a tempting location for a fugitive, and a freelance sports writer.

If she'd meant to rob him, she was even crazier than he'd figured. It was more likely that she found him suspicious and decided to do some recon. Either way, he'd have to be careful. She was prickly and distrustful and quick to draw her dagger.

He paused at the corner, listening for her footsteps. His eyes widened as he heard the sounds of another scuffle. *Damn!* Did she accost every man in her path? A sharp slap, followed by a muted female cry, spurred him into action. He sprinted down the alley, adrenaline rushing through his veins.

Isabel was standing across from a stocky man, squared up like an afternoon showdown. Her face was marred by a handprint. His side was red with blood. When the man pulled a .38 from his waistband, Brandon's world came to a grinding halt.

He didn't have time to think, or shout a warning, or second-guess his actions. He just reacted, launching himself at the guy full force and tackling him to the ground. The man's gun discharged in an earsplitting blast, and the bullet ricocheted through the alleyway, sending shards of brick flying in the air.

Weakened by the stab wound, the man beneath him didn't put up much of a fight. Brandon gripped his opponent's wrist and applied a crushing pressure, bashing his knuckles against the cobblestones. Grimacing in pain, the man released the weapon. Blood spread from his side, soaking his white shirt.

Panting from exertion, Brandon looked up at Isabel. She held her trusty dagger at an angle, letting the blade drip dry. Her eyes were dark with horror, her cheek ruddy from the blow. "Get help," he ordered.

She touched the mark on her face, glancing around warily. The police would arrive at any second, drawn by the sound of gunshot.

"Get help, now!"

She sheathed her knife, backing away.

Goddamn it. Brandon assumed that the injured man

was a cartel member, and a cold-blooded killer, but he couldn't let a stranger bleed out. *"Ayudame!"* he shouted down the alley. *"Policia!"*

She took off at a dead run.

The man underneath him lost consciousness, his head listing to the side. Brandon did his best to staunch the blood flow, cursing fluently as he put pressure on the wound. What he really wanted to do was follow Isabel.

A small crowd gathered at the end of the alleyway, and a police car arrived a few moments later, siren wailing. Two uniformed officers jumped out, shouting orders in Spanish. They crouched behind the open doors of the squad car, guns drawn.

"Manos arriba! Manos arriba!" Brandon took his red-stained hands away from the wound and held them up high, his stomach churning with dread. One of the officers rushed forward, grabbing him by the collar and shoving him facedown on the cobblestones. He winced, trying to stay still as his arms were wrenched behind his back and his wrists cuffed.

There were no Miranda rights given, no questions asked. The injured man lay motionless in a pool of blood. The officers yanked him to his feet, talking to each other in rapid-fire Spanish.

"Estaba ayudando," Brandon said. *I was helping him.*

They led him to the patrol car, ignoring his protests. "Watch your head," one of the officers said, pushing him inside.

Brandon had no choice but to cooperate. He couldn't reveal his identity without putting himself in danger. Mexican officials were often friendly, and quick to accept a bribe, but they wouldn't be so amenable if they learned his real purpose here. At this point, it was better to pretend to be a hapless surfer.

"I didn't do anything—" he said, just before the door slammed in his face.

Isabel was afraid to go back to her apartment.

She didn't know how long Carranza's man had been watching her. He might be working with a partner. Even if he'd come to Puerto Escondido solo, reinforcements could arrive anytime. Carranza would be furious to hear that she'd escaped.

She had to assume they knew everything. Where she lived, what she drove. Her only recourse was to leave town, change her name and start over.

Again.

Although she wanted to sprint, she forced herself to walk at a brisk pace, sticking to the backstreets. There was blood on her shirt, her face. Anyone who looked close would see a wild-eyed murderer.

Choking down a sob, she paused to rinse her hands in a fountain. The water ran pink, like blush champagne. Feeling queasy, she hurried on, passing through her neighborhood with her eyes averted and head down. She stopped at a locked garage several blocks from her apartment, using her key to open the door.

Months ago, when she'd decided to settle down in Puerto Escondido, she'd bought an old motorcycle from the garage owner and paid him a pittance to park it here. She'd also stashed an overnight bag in a metal drawer.

Standing on tiptoes, she reached into the drawer, locating the messenger bag. Slinging it over her shoulder, she hopped on the bike.

To her intense relief, the engine turned over.

Within minutes, she was speeding down the highway,

putting distance between her and Puerto Escondido. It was almost full dark now, and a little cooler. The wind rippled through her hair and clothes, drying her sweaty nape.

She was going to make it.

On the heels of that thought, her stomach rebelled, protesting the stress of the past hours. She pulled to the side of the road and fell to her knees, vomiting in the gravel. When her belly was empty, she dry-heaved weakly, tears seeping from her eyes.

She'd stabbed a man. Maybe killed him.

Not only that, she'd left Brandon in the lurch. Mexican officials might let him off the hook, but Carranza's men wouldn't.

"Oh, God," she moaned, fisting a hand in her hair. What was she going to do?

As soon as the nausea passed, she rose to her feet and wiped her mouth, grabbing a bottle of water from her pack. After spitting out the first sip, she drank a small amount, afraid the liquid would come back up.

Brandon had saved her life. She'd ditched him at Playa Perdida, and pulled a knife on him in the alley, but he'd stepped in to rescue her anyway. Showing zero consideration for his own well-being, he'd tackled the gunman. And how did she repay him for that gallant act? By running away.

She felt terrible.

The past two years had been harrowing, lonely and intense. She felt like she'd been dodging bullets forever. She didn't want to be a fugitive from justice anymore. And she couldn't stand the thought of another man's blood on her hands.

Head pounding, she swung her leg over the bike, gunning the engine. The problem with being on the run in Mexico was that she didn't know who to trust. Crooked officers were common because of low government wages. She couldn't go to the police, and she wasn't sure the embassies were safe. Carranza had a wide sphere of influence.

As hiding places went, this country wasn't the best choice. But she hadn't figured out who she was running from until after she crossed the border. Now she was stuck. She couldn't stay here, and she was afraid to go home.

The least she could do was try to find out what happened to Brandon. Maybe she could warn him. He might be in danger because of her, and he was obviously an innocent bystander. She felt responsible for his safety.

Decision made, she turned her bike around, driving toward the muted lights of Puerto Escondido. At early evening, the air smelled like hot asphalt and thick vegetation. Crickets chirped in unison, creating a shrill cacophony. Farther out, blue-black waves lapped at the pale shoreline, lulling the city to sleep.

Well, not the whole city. The palapa bars that raged until sunup were several blocks from Brandon's hotel. Raucous shouts were only murmurs at this distance, the music pulsing like a faint heartbeat.

She slowed her bike to a stop in a quiet area near The Pelican, taking cover behind a block wall. The spot wasn't comfortable, but it offered a decent vantage point. She could see the courtyard and the carport.

An hour later, two men in a rental car parked on the opposite side of the street. They headed to the carport first, pausing by Brandon's SUV. It was dark, so Isabel wasn't sure what they were doing. Searching his vehicle, perhaps. After a few moments, they moved on, settling down in a pair of lawn chairs in the dimly lit courtyard.

Isabel stayed hidden, her pulse racing. These were Carranza's men, without a doubt. She assumed the Mexican police would deliver Brandon to them. How could she alert him to their presence?

"Damn," she whispered, crouching lower. The longer she lingered here, the higher her chances of getting caught became. Her mind raced with options, all unpleasant. She could flee the scene or hang back and watch it unfold.

This wasn't going to be pretty.

Brandon's handcuffs were removed, along with his personal effects. Sans wallet and cell phone, he was tossed into a holding area.

He couldn't imagine a more unappealing place. It was constructed of metal and concrete. No lights or windows, no bench to sit on. A drain in the corner was the single amenity. It smelled like puke and urine.

There were two other men with him, one white, one Mexican. Both drunk.

He leaned against the wall, ignoring his cell mates. He'd never been on this side of the bars before. It was distinctly unpleasant.

After what seemed like hours, the two officers who'd collared him came back. Although he wasn't looking forward to a long interrogation, he was happy to leave the stinking confines of the jail cell.

He was led to a restroom, where he scrubbed his hands, cringing at the blood under his fingernails. They continued on to an interrogation area in the back of the building that consisted of three chairs and a scarred wooden table.

Brandon took a seat, stretching out his long legs. "Am I under arrest?"

The English-speaking cop sat across from him. "Not yet."

"How's the guy who got stabbed?"

"I can't say."

He shifted in his chair, uneasy. If the man was dead, Brandon could be looking at a murder charge. That would be a major roadblock.

"Why don't you tell us what happened?" the cop said.

Nodding, Brandon raked a hand through his hair. He didn't want to say too much, but it was always best to stick close to the truth. Someone might have seen Isabel fleeing the scene. "I was having a beer at Señor Frog's. On my way back to the hotel, I took a wrong turn and ended up in the alley. I saw a man and a woman, struggling. I thought he was attacking her. When he pulled a gun, I rushed him."

The cop frowned at the term. "Rushed?"

"I ran at him," Brandon explained. "I grabbed his arm and the bullet went flying. We fell to the ground. He dropped the gun. The girl ran away."

"Where did she go?"

"I have no idea."

"Did you stab him?"

"No," Brandon said. "I assume she did. She had the knife."

"Describe her."

Brandon hesitated, although he remembered every exquisite detail. Honeyed skin, almost-black hair, whiskey-brown eyes. He could have described the dip of her belly button and the shape of her breasts. "Small," he said, moistening his lips.

"Short?"

"No...slim. Dark hair."

"Is that it?"

Brandon pretended to think for another minute. "She was wearing a hat."

To his surprise, the officer didn't ask him any more questions. "Okay, Mr. North. That's all we need."

Relief washed over him. "I can leave?"

"Yes. We'll take you to your hotel. The Pelican, right?"

"Right." They'd asked where he was staying earlier. "Thank you." He couldn't believe they were letting him go after such a brief interview, but he wasn't going to ask for a longer visit. After his belongings were returned, the officers dropped him off at his hotel, wishing him a pleasant vacation.

Brandon thanked them again and got out of the squad car. As he approached the courtyard entrance, the hairs on the back of his neck prickled with awareness. Something wasn't right. They'd wasted his time, and then rushed him along, for a reason. What were the odds that the cops had communicated with Carranza?

He paused, weighing his options. There was no view of the courtyard or his hotel room door from this side of the street. He could circle around, through the carport, or back away and get the hell out of here.

Leaving on foot would look suspicious, and he didn't want to be without his vehicle—or the gun he'd stashed in it. Instead of playing it safe, he switched directions, heading toward the covered carport. Although it was dark inside, he could tell he was alone. He unlocked the SUV and slid into the driver's seat, putting the key in the ignition.

The engine wouldn't turn over.

Brandon tried again, frowning. It was dead.

He caught a flash of motion in the carport and realized he should have taken off running. Before he could reach for his weapon, a dark figure appeared at the driver's side, tapping on the window with the barrel of a 9mm.

Damn, damn, *damn*.

He held his hands up where the man could see them, his heart in his throat.

"Get out," the thug said, gesturing with his gun. He was tall, with rounded shoulders and a thick neck. Brandon recognized him as Gaucho Rodriguez, an enforcer for the La Familia drug cartel.

Brandon exited the vehicle, playing along. "It's all yours, bro! Take it."

Gaucho had a partner. A smaller man stood at the rear of the vehicle, studying Brandon with narrowed eyes. This was Ernestino Garcia, more commonly known as Pelón, for his balding head. Both Pelón and Gaucho were top-level members and convicted felons; they weren't here to mess around.

"We need to speak with you in your hotel room," Pelón said.

Brandon gaped at him stupidly, buying time. There was no way he'd allow this pair of miscreants to take him to a more private location. So they could tie him up and torture him for information? No, thank you.

Then again, the gun pressed to his ribs was a powerful motivator.

"Okay," he said, swallowing hard. "Whatever you say. I have the key around here somewhere…"

Pelón gestured to Gaucho, who shoved Brandon against the hood of the SUV and started patting him down. So far, so good. Before Gaucho emptied his pockets, Brandon said, "I think it's on the passenger seat."

As Pelón walked around the side of the vehicle to check, Brandon noticed a shadowy form at the edge of the carport.

Isabel.

Her presence complicated matters, but he couldn't squander this opportunity. The instant Pelón's attention was diverted, Brandon flew into motion, jamming his elbow into Gaucho's nose. It connected with a sickening crunch.

Gaucho howled in pain and stumbled back a step. Whirling to face him, Brandon kicked the weapon from his hand. It went clattering across the concrete slab, coming to rest underneath the adjacent car. Before Brandon could follow up with another punch, Gaucho charged, slamming his meaty shoulder into Brandon's midsection. Brandon landed on his back, the oxygen rushing from his lungs.

Jesus Christ. The guy weighed a ton.

He also had fists like hams. Gripping the front of Brandon's shirt, Gaucho pummeled his face, splitting his eyebrow, busting his lip. His head rocked back against the concrete with every impact. Stars exploded behind his eyes and pain blossomed in his skull, creating a brutal symphony of sound and light.

Brandon managed to bring his fist up, striking a hard blow to his opponent's ear. Stunned, and probably a little winded, Gaucho lost focus. Brandon kept swinging, connecting with his target twice more in rapid succession. Realizing he was in trouble, Gaucho slumped to the side, reaching underneath the car for his gun. Before he could close his fingers around it, Brandon scrambled upright, jumping on his back. He wrapped his arm around Gaucho's thick neck and employed a classic choke hold.

In his peripheral vision, which was growing dark, Brandon could see Pelón coming. Isabel appeared behind him, wielding a brick. She knocked him over the head with it, showing no mercy. He crumpled to the ground, unconscious.

Brandon appreciated her assistance, but he was too busy to acknowledge her. All of his energy was focused on choking the man underneath him into submission. Blood from his brow dripped into his left eye, blinding him. Finally, Gaucho's body went slack. Brandon released his grip, exhausted.

Isabel wore the same expression he'd seen in the alleyway. Fear, horror, guilt.

Sweating profusely, he wiped his face with the back of his hand and glanced at the man she'd brained. There was no blood, and his chest was moving with shallow breaths.

"Do you think he'll be okay?" she asked, nibbling a fingertip.

"I don't know," he said, rolling away from the man underneath him. "This one will wake up soon, I guarantee it."

Her eyes darted toward the street. "Let's get out of here before the police come back."

Brandon's brain felt like a scrambled egg. He was dizzy and fatigued, his mouth filled with the metallic taste of his own blood. There was no time to ask questions. Mute, he retrieved his backpack from the vehicle and they left the carport together.

She had a beat-up motorcycle parked nearby. It wasn't built for two but Brandon figured it would hold their weight. He mounted the bike first, trying to make room for her. She ended up sitting on him.

"Do you know how to drive this thing?"

"Sort of," she said, starting the engine.

The situation was surreal, like an out-of-body experience. Brandon might be able to process it in a few hours. For now, he was on autopilot, his head spinning. A minute ago, he'd been participating in a violent fistfight. Now he had a deadly female in his lap.

"I owe you one," he said, putting his arm around her waist.

She glanced around to make sure the road was clear before pressing on the gas. "We're even."

Chapter 4

The highway from Puerto Escondido to Oaxaca City wasn't for the faint of heart.

During the day, the hairpin turns, deep potholes and absent road signs kept even the most experienced drivers on their toes. At night, the journey was extremely dangerous, almost impassable.

The good news was that they were all alone.

Isabel went as fast as she dared, watching out for headlights and herd animals, feeling safer with every mile gained. Brandon voiced no complaints but she sensed his discomfort. Every time they went over a hard bump or around a sharp curve, his arm tightened around her waist and his shoulders tensed, as if he was steeling himself from the pain. He'd taken some hard knocks to the head.

She'd been surprised by the skill and ferocity of his counterattack. He'd shown no hesitation in taking on a much larger man. She still wasn't sure how he'd managed to break free. One moment he was getting pummeled, the next he was choking his opponent into submission. Isabel had watched the brutish display with a mixture of awe and unease, mesmerized by the corded muscles in his neck.

Although she'd known he was fast, she'd underestimated his strength. His lean elegance was deceptive. He fought like a professional.

She shivered at the thought. Even now, after hours on the road, she was aware of the hard thighs beneath her bottom, the locked forearm around her waist and the solid wall of his chest against her back. Well-built surfers were the rule, rather than the exception, but they didn't typically excel at ultra violence. Her mind raced with questions, and she had to force herself not to squirm on his lap.

Who the hell was he?

The noise of the engine and the speed of travel inhibited conversation. By the time the city lights of Oaxaca were visible, it was well past midnight, and Isabel was exhausted. "I'm going to find a hotel," she said as soon as they exited the highway.

Brandon made a sound of agreement. His injuries needed attention, and he had to be as tired as she was. If he wanted to take his chances at the airport, or split up, he was welcome to hail a cab from the hotel.

Finding a place to stay wasn't easy at this hour. She spotted a run-down three-story building, well off the main drag, with a private parking garage and a back exit. Luckily, there was an employee at the gate.

"Pretend you're drunk," she murmured to Brandon.

He slumped against her back, compliant.

After a brief exchange with the guard, who was happy to accept cash in exchange for a room key, she parked her motorcycle and helped Brandon up the stairs. He leaned on her, either playing drunk or because he was really hurting.

The room was cramped but clean. She flipped on the light, relieved when a ceiling fan whirred into motion. It was hot in here. At least there was a private bath, as promised. She urged Brandon toward the bed, sweat trickling between her breasts.

He sat down on the mattress, groaning as he touched his temple. Blood had matted his left eyebrow and dried in dark rivulets along his jaw. His mouth was swollen, his shirt torn. He looked like he'd lost a bar fight.

She wondered if he had a concussion, though he'd never lost consciousness. "Is anything broken?"

He rested his head against the pillows. "Just my skull."

Going to the hospital wasn't an option. "I'll try to get you some ice," she said, grabbing the bucket from the nightstand. Ice was a luxury amenity in a dive hotel like this, so she was pleased to find a functional ice maker on the bottom floor. There was also a vending machine. After returning to the room, she emptied a pillowcase and filled it with a few handfuls of ice. "Here," she said, pressing the makeshift pack to his temple.

"Thanks," he said, holding it in place.

She rummaged through her messenger bag, which had a first aid kit, complete with bandages and over-the-counter painkillers. Ripping open the square package, she offered him the two pills in her upturned palm. He washed them down with water and leaned back again, closing his eyes. His cuts needed to be cleaned, but that could wait until the pills kicked in. "Are you hungry? The vending machine has snacks."

He didn't say no, so she returned to the bottom floor to buy cold sodas, snack cakes and tortilla chips. She carried the items upstairs and set them on the nightstand. "If you want to shower, you should do it now, before I fix you up."

"You go first," he said, his lips barely moving.

She took her bag into the bathroom, eager to wash and change. The mirror was small and scratched but it reflected her unsightly appearance all too well. There was an ugly scrape on her cheek and dark circles under her eyes.

"Ugh," she said, pulling off her soiled clothes. They stank of sweat and blood and vehicle exhaust. She stepped into the shower stall and stood under the weak, lukewarm spray, her heart pounding with anxiety.

She'd stabbed a man. Killed him, maybe. Reliving the sensation of his blood gushing over her hands, she scrubbed them with a little too much vigor. Using the harsh soap, she lathered every inch of her body, trying to remove the taint of death.

Murderer, the hissing showerhead whispered. Murderer, criminal, thief.

She rinsed off and left the stall, drying her tingling skin with a nubby towel. There was a tank top and a pair of drawstring pants in her messenger bag. She dressed quickly, not bothering with a bra, and hung up her wet towel on the way out.

Brandon looked a little more alert. He'd opened his soda and finished a bag of chips. His blue eyes traveled down her body, settling on her bare toes. Her mind flashed back to the days of four-star hotels with spa services and complimentary pedicures.

"It's all yours," she said, gesturing toward the bathroom.

He rose from the bed, wincing, and picked up his pack. She moved aside as he passed by, noting that the top of his head barely cleared the doorway. At well over six feet tall, he'd have to duck down to shower.

Stomach growling, she sat down to eat. The snack cakes didn't taste very good, but the chips were okay. She devoured both, crunching noisily.

Her Beverly Hills manners were long gone, too.

When Brandon came out of the bathroom, wearing only trousers, she almost choked on the last mouthful of soda. She'd seen his bare chest at the beach. But now they were in a tiny room with a single bed, and his masculine presence seemed magnified. The smell of clean male skin permeated the space, assaulting her senses.

He blotted his eyebrow, which was still seeping, with a small towel.

Flushing, she set the empty can aside and rose to retrieve her first aid kit. "Have a seat," she said, indicating the edge of the mattress. He complied, taking the towel away from his brow as she stepped forward to treat him. She stood between his splayed thighs, her hands trembling as she cleaned the area around the cut with an alcohol square. It probably didn't need stitches; head wounds just bled a lot. "This might scar."

"Who were those guys?"

"Thugs," she said vaguely, dabbing a bit of antibiotic ointment on the cut. "Where did you learn to fight like that?"

"'Nam."

She ignored the sarcastic answer, realizing that he was annoyed with her evasiveness. It took all of her concentration to prepare a butterfly bandage without fumbling. She hadn't been this close to a man in a long time. Her breasts were inches from his face. His gaze rose to meet hers, conveying a reluctant sexual interest and faint distrust.

The feeling was mutual.

"Hold still," she said, pressing the edges of the cut together and securing it with the bandage. He sucked in a sharp breath, baring his teeth in discomfort. Then she was done, and the wound was closed up tight, almost as if she'd stitched it.

"Those guys are with La Familia," she said, sitting down next to him.

He didn't ask what that meant. The most powerful drug cartel in Mexico was infamous. "Why are they after me?"

She hesitated to give him a straight answer. Being as honest as possible was the least she could do, after dragging him into this mess, but she had to look out for herself first. "They're not after you."

His brows lifted. "They want you?"

"They want something I have."

"What?"

Isabel couldn't tell him, so she reached for the antibiotic ointment again. Using a light touch, she applied the medicine to his bruised lower lip. After so many months of deprivation, the action seemed unbearably sensual. Her nipples tightened, poking against the soft fabric of her tank top in an all-too-obvious bid for attention.

Flustered, she jerked her hand away from his mouth. "Are you hurt anywhere else?"

His lips curved into a wry smile, as if he'd thought of something amusing. Instead of sharing the joke, he made a fist, revealing swollen knuckles and a rash of small cuts. She put ointment on his knuckles and bandaged them lightly, trying to ignore the heat between them. "You don't do manual labor," she commented. His hands were strong, with ropy veins, but his palms weren't heavily callused.

A muscle in his jaw flexed. "No, but my job is physically demanding. And I teach self-defense classes on the weekends."

Self-defense classes. That explained his grappling prowess and swift reactions. "What's your day job?"

"I work for a risk management company. We test sports equipment, safety gear, anything that's designed to reduce injuries. By the way, you really should wear a helmet if you're going to surf alone at a crusher reef."

His belated advice made her feel numb. She'd probably never see that reef again. "I'm sorry for running away in the alley earlier," she said, twisting her hands in her lap. "I feel bad about leaving you with…the body."

"He wasn't dead."

She perked up. "Really?"

"They took him away in an ambulance, so he must have been alive. The police wouldn't say how he was. In any case, I appreciate you coming back. I don't think those guys had a friendly conversation in mind."

"No," she agreed, warmed by his gratitude. She began putting away her first aid supplies, self-conscious.

"Wait," he said, reaching for the antibiotic ointment. He squeezed a small amount onto his thumb and brushed it over her cheek, soothing the scrape.

Isabel's skin tingled with sensation. She was heartened by the reminder that Carranza's man had struck her first, and glad she'd been able to help Brandon fend off his attackers. She was also terrified by her response to him. Over the past two years, she'd relied only on herself. Staying away from people had kept her safe.

He made her ache for all the things she'd been missing.

His hand lingered on her jaw, framing it the way a man did before he stole a kiss. She felt her eyelids grow heavy and pulse throb. The temptation to part her lips and tilt her head back was almost irresistible.

Somehow, she found the strength to pull away. When he dropped his hand, she shoved her first aid supplies into the case and rose to her feet.

"What are your plans?" he asked.

"Get some sleep." No easy task, with him in the bed.

"Tomorrow, I mean."

She shrugged, stashing the kit in her messenger bag. Her best recourse was probably to stay in Oaxaca, lying low.

"Come to Guatemala with me."

Her gaze flew back to his, startled. "You're going there?"

"I was considering it, yeah."

"Since when?"

"Yesterday. I saw an ad for a surfing tour."

Her mind raced with possibilities. It wasn't a bad idea. Brandon was strong, he cared about her safety and he could handle himself in a fight. With his height and looks, he wouldn't be inconspicuous, but traveling couples were much more common than single women. He also had money, or access to money. Wealthy Americans were welcome everywhere in Mexico. They might be able to cross the border together.

This was her chance to escape. Should she take it?

"Those men won't give up," she warned. "Staying with me will be dangerous."

He didn't seem worried. "I assess risk for a living."

She pegged him as a controlled adrenaline junkie—and knew she could do worse. "You have a head injury."

He fingered the bandage by his left eye, deliberating. "We don't need to decide now. Let's sleep on it."

Making a tacit agreement to revisit the topic in the morning, Isabel killed the lights, settling in beside him. He didn't try to touch her again, which only increased her frustration. She was lying next to a hot gentleman, her body humming with desire. Sex was out of the question, of course, no matter how badly she wanted it. He was nursing a possible concussion, and she had to stay focused on survival.

They couldn't afford to get sidetracked.

Tomorrow night, if she decided to accompany him to Guatemala, she'd try to secure a room with two beds.

After a few minutes, his breaths came deep and even, signaling that he was asleep. Isabel relaxed slightly, her thoughts drifting. She felt safe with Brandon. Not comfortable, exactly. Their physical chemistry kept her nerves on edge, but she didn't think he'd harm her.

She also wondered why he'd offer his assistance, beyond chivalry. A man like him could have his pick of women. Those two European girls had given him the go-signal. Why would he trouble himself with a knife-wielding fugitive instead? Some guys had a thing for surfer girls; others enjoyed the chase. Many extreme sports enthusiasts were addicted to risk. Maybe Brandon was a thrill-seeker and an "exotic" female was icing on his cake.

It didn't matter, as long as he kept his distance.

She was still pondering his motives, and replaying the feel of his hand on her cheek, when exhaustion took over.

Brandon waited until Isabel fell asleep and rose from the bed, moving to the single window to stand guard.

Through the bars, he watched the dark, empty street. In a few hours, the sun would peek over the edge of the horizon, and most of the city's residents would rise for another long workday. Now, the night was quiet and peaceful.

His head didn't ache as much as it had earlier, and the nausea had passed. Judging by his blurred vision, motion sickness and general disorientation, he'd suffered a mild concussion. He should take care not to reinjure himself in the next few weeks—getting knocked out again could be disastrous. Although he didn't really assess risk for a living, he'd played enough football to know that brain damage was no joke.

He glanced back at Isabel, acknowledging that this assignment was rife with risk. Even from across the room, she tempted him. Her figure was a shadowy outline on the bed, her dark hair spilling across the pillow, chest rising with soft, even breaths. His fingers itched to sink into her hair, to skim along her slender curves. Worse, a strange tenderness welled up inside him at the sight of her peaceful slumber.

He tore his gaze away, clenching his bandaged hand into a fist. Seducing her wasn't one of his objectives. Inappropriate contact with a target was grounds for dismissal, in fact. All of his previous assignments had involved men, so that hadn't been a problem before. It shouldn't be a problem now. He'd never had trouble abstaining from sex on the job, or finding an appropriate partner during his downtime. Right now, he had no patience for abstinence and zero interest in other women. For whatever reason, he felt a very specific, intensely focused desire for Isabel. Maybe he wanted her because he couldn't have her. Or maybe he just wanted her.

Either way, he needed to get a grip.

This was a complication he hadn't anticipated. Sure, he'd admired her sexy photos—and he didn't dare conjure a mental image of the more explicit ones now, when he was feeling vulnerable—but he wasn't a horny teenager anymore. A beautiful woman with a bad personality didn't appeal to him. As far as he knew, Izzy Sanborn was a hot mess. He avoided spoiled brats and drama queens like the plague.

Isabel "Sanchez" was a far cry from the hard-partying socialite he'd researched, however. She was smart, and resourceful, and...he liked her.

He'd been trained to feel nothing for his targets, positive or negative. Hate could be as great a liability as sympathy, and he wasn't supposed to damage the merchandise. It didn't matter if they were innocent or guilty, just that they were fugitives. He didn't evaluate evidence. His instructions were to make contact, plan and execute a capture, and deliver the target unharmed.

What happened after that was none of his business.

Perhaps because Isabel was a woman, he worried about her fate. He considered the punishment she would face, and whether or not she deserved it. Questioning an assignment wasn't like him. Usually, he felt good about what he did and proud of the services rendered. He'd caught sexual predators, ruthless drug dealers, hard-core criminals. None of these men had inspired tender feelings.

Isabel wasn't a typical target, not by a long shot. Her behavior was flighty and irresponsible, but she didn't seem cruel. There were two sides to every story, and he wanted to know hers. He could tell she hadn't enjoyed stabbing a stranger, or braining a man with a brick. She wasn't a sociopath.

For the first time, he felt conflicted about his job. He should be going after those bastards in La Familia, not Isabel.

Frowning, he tested the bars on the window, which were impenetrable. The security measure was a fire hazard, and it cut off this avenue of escape. The bathroom window, facing the alleyway, was small but would do in a pinch. He wouldn't have chosen this hotel, or this particular room, if there had been others available. It was too confined.

Turning, he leaned his back against the wall, watching Isabel sleep. He studied her relaxed face, the soft sweep of her eyelashes, her slightly parted lips. Maybe he was romanticizing her situation, proscribing motives that didn't exist.

What if his instincts were off?

He'd promised his boss that an assignment was an assignment. He had no qualms about taking down a dangerous female. The deadlier the better. And backing out at this stage of the game wasn't an option.

Determined to steel himself against her allure, he vowed to collect as much information about her as possible. She was fiercely independent, a capable warrior. Although he got the impression that she didn't let anyone touch her these days, she'd seemed tempted by him tonight. If the attraction between them wasn't one-sided, he could use it to his advantage—as long as he stayed strong. He couldn't sleep with her, under any circumstances, but if he feigned disinterest, he might lose her altogether.

Walking that tightrope would be tricky, possibly torturous.

He stared at her for a long time, praying he'd be able to maintain a professional distance, wondering if she'd been wrongly accused.

She didn't look like a murderer.

Chapter 5

Izzy was lying next to a dead man.

The realization came in slow degrees as she regained consciousness. Groggy from the night before, she didn't want to open her eyes. She certainly didn't want to inspect the unnaturally stiff form beside her.

In her sleep, she'd snuggled closer, but his body offered no warmth. Instead, it sucked away her peaceful oblivion and made her stomach twist with unease. The stillness of his chest was matched by eerie silence. He wasn't breathing.

Was this really happening?

She sat up in bed, moaning as her vision swam, and then cleared. Head pounding, she forced herself to focus on the man beside her. For a few dull seconds, she couldn't place him. He was fully clothed, like her, his dark hand lying across his stomach. He looked young and well-built. There was something vaguely familiar about his slack features.

Even dead, he was handsome.

Jaime.

The events from the previous evening came tumbling back to her, a confusing blur of images and sensations. She remembered popping too many pills. Smoking too many cigarettes, ordering too many drinks.

She knew that she'd hooked up with Jaime at a seedy underground club. He was one of her favorite new friends, rich and pretty and loaded with dope. Best of all, he was always more interested in getting high than getting laid. They'd shared a cab to her Hollywood Hills apartment in the wee hours of the morning.

Everything after that was a blackout.

Fingers trembling, she reached out to touch his limp wrist. She couldn't feel a pulse, but she wasn't a nurse. When she released his hand, it stayed there, his arm sticking upright rather than falling back down by his side.

Rigor mortis.

"Oh, my God," she whispered, clapping a hand over her mouth. On the nightstand above him, there was a prescription pill bottle. She snatched it up, reading her own name on the label. These were her "knockout drops," not for casual partying.

And they were gone.

Panicking, she swept her purse off the ground and stashed the empty pill bottle inside. She had to get out of here. This was too much. Her sling-backed stilettos were lying on the shag carpet. She shoved her bare feet into them and stumbled across the bedroom, disoriented. What else should she take with her? Car keys. A light shawl. Her cell phone rested on the nightstand, message notification blinking. She couldn't think of a single person she wanted to talk to. Everyone in her current circle was a flake.

Maybe she should call a lawyer.

Her gaze skittered past the phone, settling on a brown leather bag that she knew belonged to Jaime. Although it looked like a casual briefcase for school assignments or textbooks, it housed a hefty cache of pot and cocaine.

She stared at the bag, her heart thumping in her chest, aware that it held the evidence of last night's debauchery. If she left it here, would she be charged with drug possession? Reckless endangerment? Manslaughter?

Leaving her cell phone untouched, she crouched down beside the bed to pick up Jaime's leather bag. The instant her fingers closed around the strap, a cold hand shot out, trapping her wrist in a death grip.

"Puta," the man she'd stabbed said, blood dripping from his lips.

Isabel awoke with a jolt.

She stretched her left hand across the mattress, searching for a friend or foe. Her right hand went to the knife at her waist. Both came up empty. The room's only other occupant was standing by the window, and her weapon holster had been put away last night.

The disturbing dreamscape receded as she stared into Brandon's calm blue eyes. His expression told her he hadn't missed a thing.

Self-conscious, she brought her flailing arms closer to her body. Although the temperature had cooled, her skin was dotted with perspiration, her tank top clinging to her chest. She wondered how long he'd been watching her sleep. Sitting up, she pushed her hair off her forehead.

"I wasn't sure how you'd take it," he said.

Her eyes met his, startled.

"Your coffee," he clarified, lifting his own cup.

There was another cup on the nightstand, steam rising from the top. Beside it, a mildly sweet pastry known as *pan dulce*. She took an experimental sip. He hadn't added enough sugar to suit her. "It's fine."

Satisfied, he glanced out the window, drinking his own coffee. He looked better this morning. The bruises on his face had darkened but the swelling was down. If he put on a pair of sunglasses, the flesh-colored bandage on his brow would be hard to notice. He also needed a hat to cover his ash-brown hair.

She realized that she'd made her decision. Any man who could stand watch, grab breakfast and keep his hands to himself was worth his weight in gold. She also had to admit that waking up with him was better than waking up alone, after a nightmare like that. "I'll go with you," she blurted.

The corner of his mouth lifted. "Good."

"You haven't changed your mind?"

"No." He took another drink from his cup, mulling something over.

She tore off a piece of pastry. "What is it?"

"Those guys from last night...do you owe them money?"

Chewing the bite she'd just taken, she stalled, not wanting to give away too much. "Yes, but I don't think that's what they're after."

"What are they after?"

"Blood."

His jaw tightened at the answer. "There's one thing I need to make clear before we move forward."

She regarded him warily. "What?"

"I don't like drugs. If you're on something—"

"I'm not," she said, her cheeks warming.

"Since when?"

"I haven't even had a drink in years. Is that okay with you, Boy Scout?"

"Yes," he said, curt.

She ate the rest of her *pan dulce* without really tasting it. "Why are you traveling by yourself?"

His brows rose. "Why not?"

"Are you a lone wolf?"

"This from a woman who surfs solo."

"I have reasons for that."

He lifted his cup to his lips, making a noncommittal sound.

"You're not...involved with anyone?"

"No," he said, glancing at her in surprise. "And I've never had a girlfriend who would be interested in this kind of vacation."

She sipped her coffee, contemplative. He probably dated prissy Miss America types with perfect hair. There had been a lot of those in Hollywood, if she remembered correctly. "What about guy friends?"

He shrugged. "They all have lives, and I made the plans at the last minute. Besides, I don't mind doing my own thing. Sometimes I prefer it."

Isabel tried to imagine *wanting* to be alone, and couldn't. "Do you have a family?"

"Yes."

"Are you close?" she asked, embarrassed by the sudden pressure behind her eyes. Her estranged relationship with her mother was one of her greatest regrets. She couldn't mend it from a distance, though she longed to.

His expression softened. "Yeah, we are. I'm an only child, but my parents are great. I see them almost every weekend."

Isabel felt a pang of envy. She was also an only child, bewildered by her parents' divorce, devastated by her father's death. "Sounds nice."

He gave her a measured look. "How long have you been in Mexico?"

"Too long," she said, rising from the bed. With jerky motions, she took her knife holster out of her bag and cinched it around her waist. Reminding him—and herself—that she wasn't weak or vulnerable. After lacing up her tennis shoes, she ducked into the bathroom. Bending over the sink, she scrubbed the sadness from her face. When her expression was sufficiently flat, she tied back her hair and brushed her teeth.

He rapped on the door, startling her. "They're outside."

She came out of the bathroom, her heart in her throat. "Where?"

"One in front, the other circling around back," he said, brushing by her.

Isabel couldn't believe Carranza's men had caught up with them already. She knew they hadn't followed her motorcycle last night. It was possible that La Familia had connections in this area, but unlikely.

Mind racing, she grabbed her messenger bag, crossing the strap over her chest.

Brandon shoved open the small bathroom window and stuck his head out, evaluating their only escape route. His shoulders would barely fit through. "We can get to the roof from here," he said, gesturing for her to go first.

She shut the bathroom door and stepped forward, her stomach tight with dread. They were on the third story of the building. Hanging out of this tiny window was madness. When he put his hands on her hips, their eyes locked. He couldn't promise not to let her fall, so he didn't. She appreciated his lack of pretense.

She also appreciated his strength. He lifted her like she weighed nothing, boosting her up to the windowsill. She wiggled through the narrow opening, eyes swimming at the view of the cobblestone alleyway below. It was a long way down. Already dizzy, she twisted her body around until she was sitting on the ledge.

"I've got you," he said, his arm locked around her waist.

She looked up, swallowing her fear. There was a terrace on the roof of the building, surrounded by a flimsy-looking metal railing. She had to let go of the windowsill and grab the lower edge of the railing. Hands trembling, she reached up, stretching her arms as far as she could. After a stomach-curling moment, in which she imagined a backward free fall, she grasped the railing and held tight.

"Do you have it?"

"I've got it." Praying that the railing wouldn't bend, she braced her feet on the ledge and straightened her legs, moving into a standing position on the windowsill. Brandon's grip shifted to the backs of her knees, keeping her steady. He had to release her while she climbed along the side of the building. Using every ounce of strength she could muster, she pulled herself up and over the terrace railing, which vibrated in protest.

When she was safe, her feet planted on solid ground, she wanted to collapse into a boneless heap. Instead, she peered over the railing, wondering how Brandon would accomplish the feat without help.

He stuck his head out the window, seeming relieved to see her face. His teeth flashed white in a tense-looking grin. Although the narrow opening was a tighter squeeze for his long, rangy body, the climb was easier. He reached the terrace railing and pulled himself over it with effortless grace. They started running as soon as he hit the rooftop, reaching the other side of the terrace in seconds.

The adjacent buildings were lower levels, and smashed together with no spaces between, which was typical of Oaxaca City. They offered a fast getaway.

This time, Brandon went first, climbing over the terrace railing and jumping down to the next rooftop. Isabel followed quickly, falling into his arms. Again, his hands were efficient, rather than polite—and she enjoyed the feel of them.

They took off, traversing a block of rooftops before skidding to a halt at the edge of the last building. There was another two-story within jumping distance, but its perimeter was lined with broken glass. Brown beer bottles stuck up from the black tar, jagged ends sparkling. The low-budget security measure was common throughout Mexico.

And if the glass didn't deter them, the snarling Doberman would. He bared his teeth, daring them to take the leap. A guard dog this size would deter any rooftop thief.

Brandon pulled her backward, searching for an alternative.

"There," she said, pointing at a copper pipe.

They raced over to take a better look. The skinny pipe ran along the side of the building, feeding a pair of rusted water tanks on the surface. There was no sign of their friends, who were probably still raiding the hotel room.

Brandon swung down to the next window ledge, gripping the pipe with both hands. He tested its stability by putting most of his weight on it. When it held steady, he reached for her hand. She joined him on the ledge, her head spinning.

He whipped off his belt, tying her right wrist to the metal pipe.

"What will you use?" she asked.

"I don't need anything," he said, beginning the descent.

He was taking a shocking risk, but they didn't have time to argue. While she watched him climb down, unsecured, her stomach was tied in knots. Aware that Carranza's men could show up at any moment, her eyes darted across the rooftops, down the alley.

Brandon dropped the last six feet, rubbing his palms on his shirt. The coast was still clear, so he gestured for her to hurry.

She didn't have his upper body strength at her disposal, but she wasn't burdened by his heavier muscle mass, either. The pipe was smooth, almost slippery in her hands. If his belt didn't hold, a fall from this height could break a leg, or a skull. She made her way down with painstaking care, her heart thundering in her chest. When she reached the end of the pipe, the muscles in her arms were quivering. Brandon unhitched her wrist and she let go, stumbling against him. He felt rock-solid and poised for action.

She caught a flash of movement at the end of the alley as he released her. The bigger man from last night strode toward them, his weapon drawn.

"Run," Brandon said, pushing her in the opposite direction. As they fled, a round of bullets peppered the brick siding, ricocheting across the alley. Pieces of pulverized brick exploded through the air, whizzing past her ear. Isabel lowered her head, flying around the corner with Brandon right behind her.

They faced another long, narrow street. Too long. A beat-up taxi idled about a hundred feet away, its doors open. They'd be dead before they reached it.

Cursing, Brandon pulled a gun from his waistband and shoved her back against the side of the building, away from the bullets' trajectory.

While she gaped at him, frozen with terror, he returned fire. The sound of approaching footsteps was lost in the report. Or perhaps Carranza's man had been forced to stop pursuing them and take cover.

Isabel studied the weapon in Brandon's hand, wondering where it came from. The acrid smell of gunshot residue stung her eyes and burned her nostrils. "Let's move," he said, pulling her toward the idling taxi. The driver dropped the suitcase he'd been about to load in the trunk and backed up slowly, his hands raised. Brandon kept his gaze on the cabby but spoke to Isabel. "Get in the driver's seat."

She got behind the wheel, her mind reeling. He climbed into the backseat. "Go!"

With a squeal of tires, they were off. Carranza's man came tearing down the alley, shooting wild. Luckily, none of his bullets hit their target, and Brandon didn't fire back. He was too busy holding on for dear life. Isabel took the corner so sharp he was thrown across the cab. As he righted himself, she swerved again, narrowly avoiding a head-on collision.

"Watch out!" he complained.

"Do you want to drive?" she asked, incensed.

"Damn it," he said under his breath.

"What?"

"They're following us."

Isabel glanced in the rearview mirror, noting the shiny black rental car. Within seconds, it was gaining on them. Worse, the gunman stuck his arm out the window on the passenger side, preparing to shoot.

Brandon trained his weapon on the approaching vehicle. "Go faster."

She was already punching it, testing the cab's limits. Nevertheless, she picked up speed, weaving through traffic with reckless desperation. It was a miracle she didn't hit anything. Driving in Mexico was crazy on a good day. Driving in Oaxaca City during morning rush hour with a couple of assassins following…

Well. A high-speed crash was likely.

Shots rang out, echoing in her ears. Stifling a scream, she tried to drive and duck at the same time.

"He's going for the tires," he said.

"What should I do?"

"Swerve around! Don't give him an easy target."

She did the best she could, zigzagging across lanes of traffic, passing on the wrong side of the road. As she approached a busy intersection, her entire life flashed before her eyes. The green light turned yellow, then red.

"Run it," he ordered.

She stepped on the gas, bracing herself for disaster. He leaned out the back window and squeezed off several shots. There was a terrific crash behind them as the pursuing car smashed into another vehicle.

Somehow, amidst angry honks and shrieking rubber, Isabel made it through the intersection.

She kept driving for several miles, feeling numb.

"Damn, that was close," Brandon said in a low voice. He must have decided it was safe to face forward, because he was sitting there with his eyes closed, gun beside him on the backseat, hand on his heart. His face looked pale.

She wanted to ask about his gun, but she had another topic to discuss first. "How do you think they caught up with us?"

"I don't know."

"Do you have a cell phone?" His eyes flew open. Straightening, he drew a fancy smart phone from his pocket, checking the screen. "I had to turn it in at the police station."

Isabel glanced in the rearview mirror. "Maybe they tracked it."

"Damn it," he said again. "I should have thought of that."

She didn't know why he would have. She was accustomed to danger and intrigue, and she'd overlooked it.

"Pull over right here," he said, spotting a parked bus. He hopped out of the taxi and tossed his phone onto the roof of the bus. The destination sign read Mexico City. With any luck, Carranza's men would follow it there.

When Brandon got back in the taxi, Isabel headed the opposite direction, taking a road that went to Tehuantepec. They had many miles to travel before hitting the midway point to Guatemala.

"Should we ditch this cab?" she asked.

He deliberated for a moment. They couldn't drive a stolen vehicle with distinctive markings for long. "How much gas does it have?"

She checked the gauge. "A full tank."

"I don't have enough cash to buy another car. Do you?"

"No," she said, her mouth twisting.

"If they can track my phone, they can track my credit card."

"That's probably true."

"So let's just get the hell out of town and go until it runs out of gas."

She nodded, feeling an equal measure of anxiety and relief. Carranza could influence many of the top officials, but local forces weren't very organized. They probably wouldn't launch a state-wide manhunt for a stolen taxi. Even so, Isabel stayed away from the toll roads, choosing the bumpier, less regulated freeway.

Brandon watched the blur of landscape out the side window, saying nothing.

"Where did you get that gun?"

His eyes met hers in the rearview mirror, startled. "I picked it up last night in the parking garage."

She hadn't noticed. "Does your company test hunting gear, too? Rifles, handguns…"

"No," he said, frowning. "But any good self-defense instructor knows how to use a variety of weapons."

Another reasonable explanation, she thought sourly. "I guess we're lucky that other guy wasn't as accurate as you."

"I wouldn't be so sure."

"What do you mean? None of the bullets hit us."

"You're assuming he was trying to hit us."

She kept her eyes on the road in front of her, mulling his words over. "You think those were warning shots?"

He didn't respond.

"Why would they bother?" she persisted, glancing in the rearview mirror again.

Brandon shrugged, looking straight at her. "Maybe they want more than blood."

Chapter 6

The drive to Tehuantepec was grueling.

Isabel hated sitting still for prolonged periods, especially if she was feeling stressed. Physical activity was her crutch, her comfort, her preferred method of dealing with tension. When she couldn't move around, she felt edgy and claustrophobic. Although they'd taken turns behind the wheel, Brandon didn't understand all of the road signs, so she couldn't rest. Now he was stretched out in the backseat, asleep.

She knew he had a head injury, and that he'd been up most of the night, but she was still annoyed with him for drifting off. What he'd said about La Familia wanting more than blood haunted her. She'd been sure that the man she'd stabbed in the alley had planned to kill her. Had she made a terrible mistake?

Brandon's presence bothered her even more than his words. He'd proven himself useful this morning—almost too useful. Any man in his right mind would be running the other direction after what they'd just experienced. Instead, he was sleeping like a baby, unperturbed. She glanced in the rearview mirror once again, contemplating his inelegant sprawl. One arm was bent behind his head, the other draped across his flat stomach. His T-shirt rode up, revealing a sexy whorl of hair around his navel.

She returned her attention to the road, moistening her lips. If this was his idea of fun, he had a few screws loose. Maybe that knock to the head had done some serious damage. When he came to his senses, he would leave her high and dry.

Near the outskirts of the city, she reached her breaking point. The afternoon sun shimmered on the horizon, playing tricks with her vision. They were running on fumes anyway. She pulled over next to a thick copse of trees by the side of the road.

Brandon jerked awake. "What is it?"

"We're out of gas."

He groaned, straightening his clothing as he sat up. Actually, it was more like he was adjusting his male parts, or making sure they were in the right place. She pulled her gaze away, her cheeks growing hot.

Removing a bottle of water from his pack, he took a long drink, studying their surroundings. "How far to…"

"Tehuantepec," she supplied. "A few miles."

"Let's push the cab a little farther into the trees."

She nodded, gathering her belongings from the front seat while he got behind the cab. Opening her door, she stood beside it, ready to help.

"Is it in neutral?" he asked.

"Of course."

He shoved the back end and she cranked the wheel, guiding the cab toward the heavy underbrush. Together, they wedged the small vehicle into the foliage. By the time it was found, they'd be across the border.

Brandon turned around and made good use of the trees while she found a more private spot to relieve herself. They reconvened by the side of the road, preparing to walk the rest of the way. It was blazing hot and muggy outside, typical weather for the area. As they approached the next road sign, Isabel's tank top was damp with sweat.

Tehuantepec 20 km.

"That's more than a few miles," he said in an even tone.

"The car was almost out of gas," she shot back, irritated with him, and herself, and the entire situation.

"Almost out, or out?"

She narrowed her eyes, daring him to continue this line of questioning. He wisely refrained. "I was worried about getting stranded on an open stretch of road, with no trees around to hide the cab."

He examined the highway, which was lined with lush greenery.

Isabel clenched her hand into a fist. "If you wanted to call the shots, maybe you should have stayed awake."

A muscle in his jaw flexed. "Fair enough."

But she wasn't being fair, and she knew it. "I'm sorry," she said, taking a deep breath. "I'm just tired, and hungry, and..."

...not used to being shot at, or depending on strangers.

Although she didn't say that last part out loud, he seemed to understand where she was coming from. His face relaxed and they continued moving forward. "I'm hungry, too. What do you want to eat when we get there?"

She shrugged. "Tehuantepec is pretty rustic. They'll have traditional Oaxacan food, nothing fast or fancy."

He made a sound of approval. "I'll order one of everything."

Although they kept a steady pace, the heat wore them down. The pothole-riddled roadway seemed endless. Isabel would have preferred a shorter walk, but she couldn't regret leaving the car. Sitting inside it had become unbearable.

"Tell me about your family," he requested.

"My family?"

He gave her a curious look. "Brothers, sisters, parents. You know."

"I have a mom."

"Is that all?"

She nodded, self-conscious.

"Does she look like you?"

"Yes."

"Beautiful?"

Her stomach fluttered at the compliment. Although she'd been called that, and compared to her mother many times, the words had never...soaked in...until now. "Everyone says so. She used to be an actress."

"Really? Movies or TV?"

"Both, but mostly Spanish-language horror films. Nothing you'd know of."

He looked impressed, nonetheless. And she cursed herself for saying too much. "Where were you born?"

"Santa Monica." A harmless lie. She'd been born at her dad's posh mansion in Beverly Hills, but her best memories were of the little bungalow by the pier where she'd been raised. "How about you?"

"San Diego."

She'd figured he was from California. The accent was unmistakable and he had that West Coast vibe. The fact that he wasn't an Angelino relaxed her nerves a little. Most San Diegans didn't hang out in L.A., and vice versa, so it was unlikely that she'd run into him during her party years.

"Don't tell me you're a Raiders fan."

She shook her head, sighing. "My dad was." Football wasn't on the list of American things she missed, but she wouldn't mind snuggling up next to Brandon at a game. Another impossible fantasy.

"What happened to him?"

"He died."

His brows drew together. "I'm sorry."

"It's okay," she said, and it was. In that sense, Mexico had been good for her. She'd been forced to clean up her act and *grieve,* rather than masking the pain. She could run away from the authorities, but she couldn't escape her feelings.

He talked of inconsequential things for the next few miles, the surfing spots he'd heard about in Guatemala, and his interest in the local archaeology. It finally dawned on her that he was trying to put her at ease, and that his calm attitude was deceptive. Although his natural confidence made him seem relaxed, this wasn't his idea of a good time.

"You don't have to stay with me," she said suddenly.

He looked stricken. "You think I'll ditch you on the side of the road?"

"No. But I wouldn't blame you if you did."

"I'm not going anywhere."

"I just…don't want you to feel obligated."

"I don't feel obligated."

Isabel didn't believe him, but she dropped the subject. The only other reason he could have for standing by her—sexual attraction—made her even more uncomfortable. And not because she didn't feel the pull. If he showed an interest in her tonight, she might leap on him. Or she might pass out from exhaustion as soon as she saw a bed.

It was almost dusk when they arrived, and their presence garnered little attention, as Tehuantepec didn't thrive on tourism. The bus station had closed, but the schedule was posted. They could leave bright and early tomorrow.

Hotel accommodations were few and far between. Isabel spotted an old colonial near a corner café. As they walked toward it, her stomach growled at the prospect of a sit-down dinner. Across the street, there was a small pharmacy, its lights on.

"Do you have any sunglasses?" she asked Brandon.

"No. I left them in Puerto Escondido."

"What about a hat?"

"Just a baseball cap. It's in my pack."

"Wait here," she said, ducking into the pharmacy. She found the items she needed quickly and came back out. Although he didn't ask what she'd purchased, she showed him the box of semipermanent black hair color.

"You going gray already?" he asked, studying her dark locks.

"It's for you. Your hair and eyes are too noticeable. Even with a hat on, you'll stand out from other men."

"I will anyway. I'm a head taller than the average Mayan."

"These people are Zapotec."

"Whatever. They're short."

She put the dye back in the shopping bag and handed Brandon a pair of cheap sunglasses. He donned them, smiling wryly. They weren't stylish, but they covered the bruise under his left eye and the bandage above it.

Inside the hotel lobby, she did the talking while he stood in the shadows, his hands shoved in his pants pockets. Unfortunately, there was only one room available, a single. Isabel was surprised the hotel was full on a weekday during the off-season, but she was too tired to look elsewhere. After securing lodgings for the night, they continued to the café and collapsed in chairs on the outdoor terrace, dusty and disheveled.

Brandon didn't bother with the menu. "You order for me."

She browsed the selections, which were few. "Do you like mole?"

"I like anything with meat in it."

When the waiter came, she asked him for two house specials, which included a hearty vegetable soup and fresh bread, served with green tomatillo salsa. After they devoured that, he brought two heaping plates of shredded chicken slathered in rich, dark sauce. Black mole, a staple of the area, had a bold, complex flavor with a hint of chocolate.

Brandon cleaned his plate, abandoning any attempt at conversation. Isabel smiled when he was finished, pleased that he'd enjoyed the dish as much as she had. They'd both eaten with more gusto than grace.

He leaned back in his chair, looking somewhere between satisfied and chagrined. "I think I'd have growled at the waiter if he'd passed by."

She laughed a little, taking a sip of her *agua fresca*. The light, refreshing guava juice complemented the spicy meal perfectly. "One day with me, and you've already become uncivilized."

He drank from his own glass, his mouth wry. "I wasn't that civilized before we met."

No, she thought, remembering his bared teeth and straining muscles as he choked Carranza's man into submission. He wasn't.

They fell into a charged silence, sipping their drinks

and watching the sunset fade from passion-orange to deep pink. After the day they'd had, she should have been drowsy, but the food and exercise revived her. Or maybe it was the company. When she thought about sharing a bed with him again, sleep was the furthest thing from her mind.

Brandon wasn't in a hurry to get back to the hotel room, but they had to stay out of sight as much as possible.

And staring at her from across the table was becoming a serious test of his willpower. She looked beautiful in profile, her dark hair tied at her nape. Every time she took a sip of juice, his attention was drawn to her lips. She had a delicious mouth. Her words fascinated him, too. She revealed so little about herself; it was only natural for him to crave more. She was a very sexy enigma.

"Are you ready?" he asked, tearing his gaze away from her face.

She nodded, rising to her feet.

He tossed a few bills on the table and waited for her to precede him, stifling the urge to place his hand at the small of her back. This wasn't a date. It was better than any first date he'd been on, and he'd never felt so attuned to a woman, but that didn't mean either of them were getting lucky tonight.

He wasn't used to spending every waking moment with a target, and he didn't know how to handle it. The more intelligence he gathered on Isabel, the more conflicted—and infatuated—he became. Most of what she'd told him earlier had been truthful, other than the little white lie about where she was born. It was obvious that she missed her mother. She also seemed so innocent compared to her wild child persona. Izzy Sanborn had posed boldly for men's magazines; Isabel Sanchez blushed at a simple compliment.

From what he could tell, Izzy had wielded her sexuality like a blunt object. Isabel was subtler, but no less dangerous. Her sex appeal crept up on a man, killing him with a whisper-soft caress.

They walked the short distance to the hotel and ascended the stairs. She'd secured a room that overlooked the street. When she opened the door, her face fell. It was even smaller than last night's room, with a modest bed and a set of dresser drawers.

Brandon took the space near the window, his back to her. If he looked out at the street, he could avoid looking at her.

She disappeared in the bathroom. A moment later, the shower faucet came on.

He tried not to imagine water sluicing down her naked body. Unfortunately, he'd studied photos of her in various states of undress, and he couldn't erase what had already been burned into his brain.

Groaning, he leaped to his feet and left the hotel, jogging across the street to the pharmacy. There he bought a pay-per-use cell phone and sent a quick text to his boss. He wasn't supposed to work more than twelve hours without making contact. When he returned to the hotel, she was still in the bathroom. The sound of the shower faucet morphed into a faint sloshing of water. After puzzling over it for a few seconds, he realized she was washing something in the sink, probably clothing. A few moments later, she came out wearing a towel.

"It's all yours," she said, nodding at the bathroom. She clutched the towel to her chest, holding a small bundle of wet clothes.

He took a cold shower that didn't cool him off in the

least. Taking Isabel's lead, he scrubbed his shirt and shorts with bar soap. Hanging the shirt up to dry, he put the shorts back on, along with his dusty cargo pants. There was no sense in washing a pair of trousers that wouldn't dry by morning.

Isabel knocked on the door. "Brandon?"

He gave himself a warning look in the mirror before he answered. *Don't touch her.*

Because of their respective heights, her eyes were level with the center of his chest as he opened the door. His muscles tightened on instinct. She dragged her gaze up to his, a pulse in her throat fluttering. "Do you want to use this hair dye?"

He didn't want that crap in his hair. Or her hands on him, for that matter. His nerves were as taut as a bowstring, and she looked like a wet dream in that damp towel. He moistened his lips, studying her smooth, suntanned skin.

"It's the cheap kind, so it probably won't last long," she said. "And you can always get it removed in the States."

Anything that helped them blend into the crowd was worth it, so he nodded his assent, standing aside to let her in. While she mixed the ingredients in a small plastic tray, he took a seat on the closed lid of the commode. He examined the terry cloth knot between her breasts, half hoping it would come undone. Tendrils of dark hair clung to her neck, leaving beads of water on her bare shoulders.

There were mental tricks he'd learned, survival techniques in the event of capture and torture. With a little effort, he could direct his mind elsewhere. But he didn't. He stared at the hem of her towel, mesmerized. If he inhaled deeply enough, maybe he could catch a trace of her sweet female scent.

"Your face looks better tonight," she murmured.

His eyes rose to meet hers, curious.

"The bruises, I mean."

He touched the bandage at his temple.

"I'll leave that on another day. Unless it's bothering you."

"No," he said, dropping his hand.

"Good." She stepped forward, wielding a tray of dye and a little brush. "I have to do the edges first."

He sat still while she applied black gunk to his hairline. She was much too careful, as if worried about displeasing an important customer. Biting her lower lip in concentration, she brushed on the dye, making him tilt his head this way and that. When this first step was completed, she put on a pair of clear plastic gloves and got down to business. Grabbing a small handful of paste, she worked it into his hair.

Brandon expected to have trouble with her proximity, but he hadn't anticipated enjoying her touch so much. It felt like she was massaging his head, caressing him with circular motions. Tantalized by the fact that her body was naked under the towel, and her breasts mere inches from his face, he couldn't control his response. She was standing between his open thighs, her legs bare all the way up to *there*. If her towel fell open a few inches…

He groaned, clenching his hands into fists.

"Does your head still hurt?" she asked, pausing in concern.

"No."

She gentled her touch anyway, killing him softly. He couldn't have been more aroused if she'd been stroking his erection. It was as though his scalp had a direct connection to his groin, and his entire body reacted, his gut tightening, spine tingling.

Weakened by desire, he allowed the nearly nude photos

of her to spring to the forefront of his mind. There was one picture in particular that stood out to him as painfully erotic. She'd been straddling a surfboard in a fishnet bikini. Her right hand was draped across her breasts, left cupped over her sex. Without their strategic placement, the photo could have been called pornographic.

She finished the job and stepped back, studying her work. "Good thing your eyebrows are kind of dark."

His beard stubble came in dark, too, although it wasn't anywhere near black. He might have to shave if the difference was glaring.

Removing her gloves, she tossed the mess into the trash. After waiting a few minutes for the dye to set, she said, "Put your head in the sink."

He leaned over and let her rinse the excess dye from his hair. When he straightened, she rubbed a dry towel over his head and left it hanging around his shoulders. Then she retreated, giving him room to stand. "See how it looks."

"I don't care how it looks."

She flinched at his gruff tone, totally unaware of the effect she had on him.

His gaze wandered from her frowning mouth to the terry cloth knot between her breasts, analyzing the resistance of both barriers. Her confusion faded into understanding and she stilled, sucking in a sharp breath. He remained silent, letting her decide what to do about their predicament. She could walk away. He couldn't even stand.

Moistening her lips, she brought a trembling hand to her chest. For a quick, hot second, he thought she might let the towel drop. He pictured her untwisting the terry cloth and standing naked before him, offering herself. In the next heartbeat, he'd have her legs around his waist and her back against the wall.

But she didn't loosen her towel; she clutched it tight. "I can't."

That made two of them. "Why not?"

Her throat worked as she swallowed. "It's complicated."

His raging hormones disagreed. They said it was as easy as unbuttoning his trousers and urging her down on his lap.

"I like you—"

"I like you, too."

Her eyes filled with anguish. "You don't even know me."

"Then let me get to know you," he said, frustrated. "Why won't you tell me what those assholes want? What have you done that's so bad?"

She let her shoulders rest on the wall behind her, staring up at the ceiling. "They think I killed someone."

"Did you?"

Her gaze reconnected with his. "I don't know."

"How can you not know?"

"I was drunk. And high. I—feel responsible."

He believed her. "This happened in the U.S.?"

She crossed her arms over her chest, refusing to say more.

He wanted to advise her to go to the police, and promise to help her, but that kind of conversation wasn't permitted in his line of work. Tipping off a subject was an egregious offense, worse than seducing one.

And, although he felt certain that she wasn't a cold-blooded murderess, he couldn't trust her not to hit him over the head and bolt.

When he'd recovered well enough to stand, and to touch her without losing control, he rose to his feet. Cupping her chin with one hand, he tilted her face up to look at him. "Let's try to get some rest," he said, brushing his lips over hers, very gently. "Trust me on this. Everything will be okay."

Her eyes shone with tears, but she nodded, accepting the lie as easily as he'd told it. They turned off the lights and climbed into bed, both longing for what they couldn't have. Almost an hour later, her breathing turned soft and steady. He rose from the bed to stare out the window, feeling twice as conflicted as the night before.

Chapter 7

Isabel woke at dawn.

Once again, Brandon's side of the bed was empty. He was standing in the dim light by the window, looking down at the street below. *"Buenos días,"* he said in a gruff voice, glancing over his shoulder at her.

The towel she was wearing must have fallen away as she slept, because she was naked beneath a thin sheet.

Sometime during the night, he'd covered her.

She sat up, clutching the sheet to her chest. Had he looked his fill before leaving the bed? Maybe it had been too dark to see anything until now.

"Did you sleep well?" he asked.

"Yes," she said, flushing a little. Last night she hadn't been plagued by nightmares of dead and dying men. A very healthy, very vibrant fantasy of Brandon had invaded her dreams instead. Her tummy quivered at the possibility that she'd moaned his name or writhed against him, insensible.

"I don't think the café is open," he said, "but we can buy breakfast from a street vendor on the way to the bus station."

She nodded, wondering how to get up without exposing herself further. Her towel was draped over the edge of the mattress, but she couldn't put it on without letting the sheet drop. He followed her gaze, understanding the dilemma.

Her heart skipped a beat as their eyes met and held. He stared at her a moment, studying her bare shoulders and disheveled hair. Then he turned back to the window, offering her a modicum of privacy.

She scrambled off the bed, wrapping the towel around her and grabbing the clothes she'd hung up the night before. They weren't quite dry. In the bathroom, she used the facilities and changed quickly, her skin prickling with gooseflesh. She'd kill for new lingerie and a pretty sundress. Instead she had two sets of clothes; one dirty, one damp. Her plain white bra and pink cotton panties were serviceable, at best. She put on her baggy drawstring pants and worn gray tank top, grimacing at her reflection in the mirror. It didn't help that the mark on her cheek had faded into a sickly greenish bruise.

After brushing her teeth, she pulled her hair into a knot at the nape of her neck and left the bathroom.

Brandon's appearance was also scruffy, but he managed to look sexy and dashing and a little bit dangerous. His jaw was unshaven, his shirt wrinkled. Although the black hair and cheap sunglasses didn't quite suit him, she was pleased with the results. Sitting down on the bus, he would blend in with the crowd. "Ready?"

She slung her messenger bag across her shoulder and

followed him out the door. Unlike Oaxaca City, where the daily grind started early, Tehuantepec was a quiet village of textile weavers and tradesmen. They walked toward the bus station in silence.

It was hard to believe they'd been involved in a high-speed chase yesterday morning. She hoped the next leg of the trip was less eventful.

Walking down the deserted road, Isabel felt uneasy. The conversation they'd had last night shouldn't have happened. He knew too much about her already. Perhaps because of the close calls they'd faced, she'd bonded with him emotionally. She wanted to tell him her secrets, ask him to hold her...let him help her.

But she couldn't relax her guard. He was risking his life by traveling with her. He'd accepted that, and she'd been honest about the danger. As long as she kept him in the dark with regards to her true identity, he'd be able to walk away unscathed. La Familia couldn't drill him for information he didn't have.

Every time she revealed a detail about her past, she made it easier for Brandon to find out who she was. With a little effort and a basic internet connection, he could discover her name, notify the authorities and cause a lot of trouble for them both.

Isabel regretted many of the decisions she'd made leading up to this point, and she agonized over her next step. For the past two years, she'd been trapped in Mexico, putting her life on hold. She couldn't move forward or turn back. Now she had the opportunity to break free. What would she do with it?

If she turned herself in, she'd probably go straight to jail, trading one miserable existence for another.

And if she didn't, she was destined to keep running forever.

The bus station was busier than she'd anticipated, and the terminal was filled with early-morning passengers. She bought third-class tickets, the only kind available in many rural areas, to Tapachula. From there it would be a short trip to Guatemala.

While they waited for their bus to board, she paid for a cup of yogurt at the snack shop. Brandon bought a ham and cheese torta from a female vendor on the sidewalk, washing it down with fresh-squeezed orange juice.

"How long will it take to get to there?" he asked.

"All day."

"Can we cross the border tonight?"

She shrugged. "It depends on the bus schedule. We'll probably have to wait until morning."

He didn't ask what they would do after they crossed the border, assuming they made it that far. The La Familia drug cartel was determined and resourceful. They had no qualms about bribing the authorities or harming innocent people. Isabel hoped Carranza's men were on a wild-goose chase to Mexico City, but she couldn't bank on it.

"We'll be entering an area called the Isthmus," she said. "There are rebel soldiers here, and all throughout Chiapas, so the government has its own men patrolling the area. We can expect military checkpoints and routine searches."

He emptied his container of juice. "Great."

"Foreign travelers have been sympathetic to the rebels, so they're often targeted for questioning."

"And for handouts?"

"Yes," she said, inclining her head. "Like the local police, military men will accept money when it's offered."

"That's a polite way to describe highway robbery."

She stiffened, getting defensive. These weren't her people, but after several years in Mexico she felt compassion for them. "Most government employees can't afford to feed their families on the wages they're paid. Do you know that mailmen work for tips? Hunger, not greed, is the real motivation."

He smiled easily, his teeth a brilliant flash of white. "Sounds like you're a rebel sympathizer."

The teasing accusation caught her off guard. She'd been too busy looking out for herself to worry about politics or human rights. On the other hand, the Mexican government's corruption had sealed her in quite neatly, and she resented that. If La Familia had less power, she'd have more freedom. "I have enough problems of my own."

He couldn't argue that point.

"If we're questioned, let's say our passports got stolen," she continued. "We'll pose as a couple on vacation. I'll be...Maria Garcia."

"Am I Mr. Garcia?"

"Whatever. Pick a first name."

"Ben."

She committed it to memory and they worked out a few more details, waiting until the bus was about to leave before boarding. If the authorities were looking for them, specifically, it wouldn't matter what they said, but it made her feel better to have a plan in place. As the bus pulled away from the station, she glanced around for suspicious characters. The other passengers appeared to be regular people on their way to work. Every few miles, the driver collected more. Soon the bus was full.

Isabel had become accustomed to this mode of travel. She liked listening to the friendly chatter of passengers and watching the landscape change. The road to Tapachula was scenic, marked by rolling hills and rocky cliffs. But on a day already fraught with tension, these elements were hardly relaxing.

Unflappable as ever, Brandon made a pillow out of the

crook of his arm and leaned his head against it, ready to drift off.

She noted that he looked tired, rather than bored. "Did you sleep last night?"

"I was letting you sleep."

Her mouth dropped open. "What about the night before?"

He made a noncommittal sound, drowsy.

She calculated the hours he'd dozed in the back of the cab as two or three, at the most. No wonder he was exhausted. Although it was smart to rest in shifts, with one person standing watch, Isabel was annoyed with him for taking the sole responsibility. Who did he think he was, her bodyguard? More importantly, how much time had elapsed after her towel slipped off, and before he covered her?

A flush crept up her neck as she thought about him ogling her while she slept. Last night, in the bathroom, he'd wanted her. His eyes had burned with it, his face stretched tight across his cheekbones. She hadn't been aware of his interest at first. His reluctance to stand had been a clue, and his heated gaze another, but he hadn't tried to touch her.

Why?

Having sex with him was a bad idea; the situation was complicated enough. Even so, the chemistry between them was sizzling and she longed to act on it. If he'd kissed her, rather than initiated a conversation, she probably would have melted in his arms.

It had been so long—she might have exploded.

While he slumped against the window, his breathing deep and even, she squirmed beside him, restless and frustrated. Brandon struck her as a man who knew his way around the ladies. He assessed risk for a living. Surely he understood that making a move had a higher success rate than asking permission. Either he didn't think she was worth the effort, or he had serious reservations about going to bed with her.

How conceited she'd been to assume his motives were sexual! She'd enjoyed believing he would endanger his life for a chance to get in her pants. Apparently, he'd rather admire her nude body from afar than touch it with his bare hands.

Maybe he just wasn't that into her.

She studied him from beneath lowered lashes, irritated by his mystique. His sunglasses were still on, his head resting against his bent arm. His other arm was draped across his lap, obstructing her view. She wished she'd done a more thorough examination of his manly parts last night, when he'd most assuredly been aroused.

With a heavy sigh, she pulled her gaze away from him. It was useless to blame Brandon for not trying hard enough to seduce her. She was the one who'd said no. What would have happened if she'd removed her towel instead? He might have taken her against the wall, right then and there.

Shivering at the idea, she pulled her notebook out of her messenger bag. Reading over the article she'd outlined just two short days ago made her heart ache with regret. Once she crossed the border into Guatemala, there'd be no turning back. If she purchased fake documents, she could keep traveling, but she'd never see Playa Perdida again.

She doodled in the margins, her thoughts drifting. Instead of penning an ode to surfing or a standard travelogue, she fantasized about rewriting history. In her former life, she might have fallen for Brandon at first sight. She pictured a handsome young man and a flirty young woman meeting on a deserted beach. They enjoy an amazing surf session and she accepts his offer to have lunch. Then he invites her to lounge at his hotel pool. They sip piña coladas all afternoon…and she passes out drunk.

Isabel scribbled over her drawing of an umbrella-topped beverage and tore the page from the notebook, crumpling it up.

Maybe her reasons for avoiding intimacy were just as complicated as Brandon's. She'd never had sex sober. Most of her encounters had been sloppy and soulless, hard to remember, best forgotten.

Inside, she still had the same insecurities. The emptiness that had compelled her to seek male attention was still there. But now she couldn't dull her inhibitions with drugs and alcohol. She wasn't a party-loving, barely legal bad girl anymore, either. Sex with Brandon might be an awkward disappointment for both of them.

While she pondered this disturbing crux of her life, in which all of her problems seemed to have collided into one another, Brandon slept on. They passed smog-burping mescal factories and endless rows of agave. She could almost taste the sharp, smoky flavor of the potent liquor they produced.

Finally they arrived at Arriaga, a midsize industrial no-man's-land. The bus driver announced a thirty-minute break for refueling. Brandon roused at the sound of the intercom, glancing around.

"Let's go," she said, dying to stretch her legs.

He shrugged into his backpack and followed her down the aisle, ducking his head as they exited the bus. After using the restrooms, they strolled through the open market, browsing the local crafts and produce stands. He bought some snacks for the road and she selected a coconut Popsicle, unwrapping it on the way back to the bus stop.

"Do you want to switch seats?" he asked.

Nodding, she preceded him. Her butt was already numb from sitting, but it was nice to have a window view. She expected him to slouch down and fall asleep again. Instead, he watched her eat the Popsicle, moistening his lips.

She licked a creamy drop from the underside. "Want some?"

A flush crept up his neck. "No thanks." It was almost noon, and incredibly hot inside the bus. She could see sweat gathered at his hairline and feel the heat of his body next to hers. Although he smelled like deodorant and hotel soap, some of the other passengers sported an earthy, unwashed odor.

Turning her face to the window, she finished her Popsicle. The scent of hard work and soiled clothing and even farm animal by-products didn't bother her so much these days, but she preferred a clean breeze.

"Why did you start surfing?" he asked, out of the blue.

She put the Popsicle stick away and took a quick sip of water, contemplating the question. "I grew up a few blocks from the beach. There were always surfers walking down the sidewalk in front of my house. I never got tired of watching them on the waves."

"And you wanted to learn?"

"Not at first. My mom wasn't the sporty type, and I wanted to be just like her, so it didn't occur to me to try until I was eleven or twelve. Then I started noticing the surfer girls—and how much attention they got from the boys."

He smiled, acknowledging this universal truth. A bikini-clad female with a surfboard turned heads everywhere she went.

"My dad bought me a pink shortboard one summer, and he paid for lessons. He was so proud when I won my first contest." The memory was bittersweet, because her parents had disagreed about her involvement in the sport. Her father had encouraged her to travel the world, reach for the stars. Her mother had wanted her to stay home, be safe. "Later that year, he got remarried, and..."

"What?" he pressed.

She lifted one shoulder. "He didn't visit anymore."

His mouth twisted with derision. "That sucks."

"Yeah. He didn't visit much before—they'd been divorced since I was five—so I was thrilled by his interest. I kept surfing, and winning, thinking if I just tried a little harder, did a little better, he'd come back again."

"But he didn't?"

"No. Never."

"What an asshole."

She laughed a little, agreeing with him. But her eyes felt hot and her throat tight, because after all these years, it still hurt. "How about you?" she asked, lobbing the question back at him. "Why did you start surfing?"

He rubbed a hand over his jaw. "My mom surfs."

"No way," she said, delighted.

"She taught me the basics when I was a kid."

"That's the cutest thing I've ever heard."

Groaning, he lifted the lenses of his sunglasses to massage his eyes. "I knew I shouldn't have told you."

She laughed again, reassessing his appeal. With his strong features, rock-hard body and rumpled appearance, *cute* wasn't the first word that came to mind. But, like it or not, he seemed to have developed a sensitive side, along with a delicious set of muscles, and that didn't take away from his masculinity in the least.

If anything, it made him more attractive.

"My dad's athletic, too, but his sport is football," he said.

"And you do both?"

He nodded. "I played ball in college but wasn't pro material."

Forcing herself to look away, she stared out the window once again. He abandoned the conversation and dug into his backpack, finding a magazine to read. She did a double take when she saw the cover: *Wave.*

"Where did you get that?" she asked, breathless.

"On the newsstand in San Diego," he replied. "Why?"

Her first article, "Lost Beach," was published inside. She hadn't received an author copy and she'd never seen her words in print before. "I heard they were doing a piece on Puerto Escondido."

"They did," he said, flipping to the right page. "Check it out."

Trying not to appear overeager, she accepted the magazine, her heart racing as she pored over the glossy pages. The two-page spread had several wide-angle shots of Playa Perdida, taken by a professional photographer. In bold italics, an insert read, "I'm alone in the barrel. It's a jade-green hollow, deadly tropic, filling my soul with exhilaration."

Her lips parted with pleasure, her eyes soaking up every detail.

"Good, right?"

Realizing he was watching her intently, she attempted to school her features into a less ecstatic expression. "Do you think so?"

"It inspired this vacation."

"Really?"

He nodded. "I had some time off and I wanted to take a surf trip. I was considering Mexico but dismissed Puerto Escondido as too well-known, and a little too big, to be honest. After I read the article, I changed my mind."

Isabel couldn't imagine a nicer compliment to her work. "What about it appealed to you so much?"

Leaning close to scan the pages, he said, "The idea of doing something totally original and a little bit crazy, I guess. There's a line about what it means to be on top of the world if no one's around to see it. I could relate to what he was saying about self-validation and getting away from the crowd."

"He?" she repeated.

Brandon looked up from the text. "What?"

"The article is anonymous."

"Oh, right." He settled back in his seat, regarding her with curiosity. "You think a woman wrote it?"

Damn her impertinent tongue. She closed the magazine, shoving it toward him. "I don't have any idea."

"It has a masculine slant. 'Conquering virgin territory, riding untried waves.'"

"You're reading too much into it," she said, flustered.

He seemed amused by the charge. "Am I?"

"Of course. Sexual metaphors are common in male-dominated sports."

"Ah. You think we should avoid making innuendoes about riding an oblong structure into a sleek hollow?"

Her lips twitched at the image he painted. "Make all the innuendoes you want, but it doesn't change my experience. I've never felt like I was getting it on with the ocean, or screwing my surfboard."

"You screw the ocean *with* the surfboard."

"Maybe *you* do. I just surf."

He laughed, shaking his head. "There's another reason to assume the article was written by a man. Female athletes are much less likely to take unnecessary risks. The only woman I know who would paddle out alone in a place like that is—"

Isabel's stomach sank as he broke off, connecting the dots. She cursed silently, aware that she'd given herself away.

In the next instant, she realized that Brandon had stopped talking for a different reason. The bus had arrived at a military checkpoint, and uniformed soldiers were poised to step on board for a routine inspection.

She froze in her seat, trapped.

Chapter 8

Brandon slouched down and adjusted his baseball cap, tugging the brim a little lower on his forehead.

"Let me do the talking," he said as two soldiers climbed the steps at the bus's front entrance.

Isabel, whose lips had drained of color, didn't argue. Although her Spanish was far superior and she understood the local idiosyncrasies better than he did, he couldn't let her take the lead. If these men performed a thorough search of his belongings, they'd find a lot more than a gun strapped to his ankle. There were several layers of deception to strip away. He was posing as Ben Garcia. Brandon North was another alias. He had documents on his person with his real last name on them—Knox—but he couldn't brandish them before they crossed the border. Doing so would endanger both their lives.

The first soldier looked about eighteen. He made his way down the aisle, a hard expression on his smooth young face. Isabel caught his attention, but he didn't give Brandon more than a cursory glance.

The second soldier wasn't quite as green, and Brandon prayed that his agenda didn't include shaking down tourists or searching for fugitives. This man, even his entire squad, might have a picture of Isabel in their back pockets, courtesy of Manuel Carranza.

The uniformed officer noticed Isabel the same way his partner had, with a flicker of male appreciation but no special interest. So far, so good. His gaze moved to Brandon, assessing his long legs and European-made hiking boots.

"Citizenship?" he asked in heavily accented English.

There was no sense in lying. "U.S."

"Passport?"

Brandon decided to stick to Isabel's plan of claiming their passports had been stolen. Although the military probably didn't have photos or detailed descriptions of them, their names could be listed as persons of interest. "Can we talk about that outside?" he asked, exchanging a worried glance with Isabel.

The soldier agreed, stepping aside to let Brandon pass. Bribes were always better brokered away from prying eyes. While they escorted him out the back entrance, Isabel stayed in her seat, quiet and still. Ready to bolt.

As they exited the bus, Brandon gave the soldiers his best clueless American impression. "I don't have my passport, man. Almost all of our stuff got stolen in Oaxaca City."

The younger soldier had no idea what Brandon had just said. The older one appeared to understand the important parts. "No passport?"

"I know we need to get it taken care of, but I didn't want to screw up our itinerary by traveling back to the embassy in the middle of our vacation. I told my girl it would be okay to wait a few days and now she's going to freak out. Can you give me a break?"

"Remove your bag and open it," the older soldier said, impatient. He either didn't believe Brandon's excuse or didn't care.

Complying with the orders, Brandon shrugged out of his backpack and unzipped the main compartment, which had nothing he needed to hide—from them, anyway. "Let's make a deal," he said, leaving the *Wave* inside and pulling out a men's magazine. The first soldier's eyes widened when he saw the lingerie-clad female on the front cover. The second was more interested in the pair of twenties Brandon slid between the pages.

"My girlfriend is already pissed," he said, wondering if Isabel was using this opportunity to shimmy out a side window and run into the jungle. "You'll be doing me a favor by taking this skin mag off my hands. If she sees it I won't get laid for a week."

The soldiers rifled through the rest of backpack, ignoring his bribe attempt. Brandon's stomach tightened with unease. Refusing to submit to a search and seizure wasn't an option in Mexico, but he couldn't allow them to pat him down. Pulse racing, he calculated the odds of drawing his weapon.

Not good.

He'd have to start running. These men knew the area, so they'd catch him easily, but the disturbance would give Isabel a chance to slip away. For the first time in his life, he considered jeopardizing the mission to protect his target.

To his intense relief, extreme measures weren't necessary. After checking his backpack for illegal contraband, the soldiers didn't hassle him further. The older officer took the money, handing his partner the magazine. Both appeared satisfied. They advised Brandon to report his stolen passport to the U.S. consulate and sent him on his way.

He got back on the bus, sweating bullets, and took his seat next to Isabel. A moment later the bus pulled away from the checkpoint.

She held herself tense beside him, her hands twisted in her lap. He didn't fool himself into thinking she'd been concerned for his welfare. While he'd been contemplating risking his entire career for her, she'd been plotting a quick escape. He knew she'd ditch him in a heartbeat if she felt threatened.

She leaned closer, her lips almost touching his ear. "What did you give them?"

Damn his traitorous body for reacting. "Forty dollars and a dirty magazine."

After a brief pause, she asked, "How dirty?"

"Dirty enough," he said with a harsh laugh, removing his sunglasses. Isabel was featured in the magazine they'd accepted as a bribe, and the photos inside were very provocative. She was wearing striped knee socks and tiny white panties with a cropped T-shirt, her hair in a cute ponytail. The effect was sporty and girlish and very Lolitalike. He felt a little perverted for responding to it.

Having that particular issue among his possessions, along with the new edition of *Wave,* was too big of a coincidence to explain away.

But getting rid of it also put them in jeopardy. If Carranza had employed the government's help to find Isabel, and Brandon was fairly certain that was the case, it was only a matter of time before they tracked her down. The taxi near Tehuantepec would be discovered. Military personnel would be questioned about unusual foreigners. The magazine might get passed around the office, or make its way into enemy hands.

Brandon wished he hadn't been carrying it.

"We can't stay on this bus," she said.

"Agreed." It would be best to find another mode of transportation altogether.

"Do you have anything against hitchhiking?"

"Nope."

Several hours passed before they arrived at the next town, and Brandon didn't get any more rest during this leg of the trip. He kept glancing back, expecting to see military trucks or flashing lights. Isabel stayed stiff and silent in her seat. She probably regretted their previous conversation about her "anonymous" article.

Brandon had always found it easy to gather personal information from his targets; people loved to talk about themselves. Often, the details were uninteresting or distasteful. He filed them away for future reference, unmoved. With Isabel, every facet of her life fascinated him and he couldn't distance himself from her emotionally. The more he knew of her, the more he wanted to know. And he'd begun to resent the role he was playing.

They exited the bus with the other passengers and started walking down the highway. Brandon felt dangerously exposed. It was also muggy as hell. Judging by the clouds gathering on the horizon, they were in for rain. He wouldn't mind an afternoon shower, cooling his overheated skin and washing the stink of the bus away.

Luckily, the rules of hitchhiking worked in their favor. Couples had a higher success rate than single men, and attracted safer rides than single women. In Mexico, stranded tourists were a welcome sight—they usually had cash.

A small car pulled over for them in no time. *"Adonde van?"* the driver asked.

"Tapachula," Isabel said.

With a jerk of his chin, the driver invited them to climb in. There was a woman with a baby on the passenger side. She stepped out to give them access to the backseat, offering a friendly smile. The space was cramped, one side stacked high with woven blankets and shawls. Brandon tried to scoot over, but he couldn't make room for Isabel. He couldn't really fit himself; he was too tall to sit comfortably in most economy cars.

Once again, she ended up on his lap.

He spread his knees wide to accommodate her. She settled in, perching on one thigh rather than snuggling up to his crotch. When the driver's wife returned to the passenger seat, they were all wedged in tight.

"Están bien?" the driver asked, making sure they wanted to ride this way.

"Sí," Isabel replied, shifting her weight on him. Their only other option was to walk along the road and wait for another car.

The driver stepped on the gas and turned the radio on, blasting something that sounded like Spanish-language country music. The noise served to insulate them further. Brandon clenched his teeth and prayed for strength. During the long motorcycle trip to Oaxaca City, his aching head had prevented him from enjoying the feel of her body. A different sort of discomfort was bothering him now. Although she made an effort to avoid direct contact, bracing her arms against the seat and balancing on his thigh, her struggles were in vain. Heat and intimacy swelled between them. She smelled of cheap bar soap and sultry female perspiration. He caught a hint of coconut on her breath and smothered a groan.

Don't think about—

Too late.

Last night, he'd watched the towel creep up her thighs as she slept. It fell away from her breasts first, draping across her flat tummy. Her nipples were soft and dusky, so tender-looking he wanted to weep. Then she rolled over, treating him to a view of her shapely bottom. It looked firm and supple and smooth as silk.

And now, that part of her was teasing his erection. Because she was sitting at an angle, her body half-turned toward him, he suffered the additional agony of her breasts in his face. With every bump in the road, and there were many, she rocked against him.

He was sweating like crazy, but so was she. The car had no air-conditioning, and very little breeze made its way to the backseat. While he watched, a tiny drop rolled from the hollow of her throat, nestling between her breasts.

It was embarrassing to be this turned on when there were three strangers in the car—one of them a *baby*. Isabel had to be aware of his arousal, because she wouldn't meet his eyes. The car lurched over another speed bump, throwing them together. Her breasts jiggled from the impact, nipples jutting against the thin cotton tank top. His gaze moved from that gorgeous flesh to her lovely face, noting that her cheeks were flushed.

God, she was hot.

Instead of apologizing for his hard-on, or pretending it wasn't there, he repositioned her on his lap, letting her feel all of him. After a moment of resistance, she reclined her body, resting her head on his shoulder. Neither of them was relaxed; he could feel her rapid breaths and quickened heartbeat. But at least they were acknowledging the need between them. Maybe now it would go away.

She held herself very still, as if trying not to squirm against his erection. He tried not to picture her in a fishnet bikini, the fabric playing peekaboo with her taut nipples, exposing the slick folds between her thighs.

Nope. Not going away.

He smoothed his palm over her belly, feeling it quiver. She covered his hand with her own, pressing tight. With his other hand, he laced his fingers through hers. They stayed locked together, trembling and desperate, for what seemed like an eternity.

Finally, his erection subsided a little, and her tension eased. He thought she might fall asleep on him. If the rhythmic jostle of the highway hadn't been broken up by annoyingly random speed bumps, he might have drifted off himself.

As they approached Tapachula, Brandon started to come back to his senses. The blood was circulating to his brain again.

Staying in Chiapas was out of the question. They had to cross the border tonight. After another close call with the authorities, they couldn't afford to stop moving. There was also no way he could continue to keep his hands off her if they shared another tiny hotel room. The temptation to toss her down on any available surface, and throw his career out the window, was overwhelming.

He didn't give a damn about delivering the goods anymore. He just wanted to get at her. There was nothing he wouldn't do to her. Nothing.

When the driver turned his radio down, Brandon gave Isabel a gentle shove, moving her pert bottom away from his distended fly. *"Van a Guatemala?"* he asked, hoping they could travel straight through.

"No. *Está cerrado.*"

Brandon frowned. Guatemala was closed?

"The road is closed," Isabel interpreted for him. "Why?"

"Por la festía."

Her expression was blank for a moment before she clapped a hand over her forehead. "Today is All Saint's Day."

"Sí," the driver's wife said, patting the baby, who had started to fuss.

Isabel stared at Brandon. "And tomorrow is *día de los muertos.*"

"What the hell does that mean?"

"Day of the Dead. There will be a festival, parade, processions...."

"Will the road be closed tomorrow, too?"

The driver nodded, claiming there would be no through traffic in Tapachula for the next two days. He considered this a happy coincidence. His wife sang the praises of the celebration, claiming it attracted visitors from all over Mexico and Central America.

"I'm sorry," Isabel said to Brandon, chagrined. "I didn't even think of it. Day of the Dead is a very popular holiday on the Isthmus, like Christmas. The townspeople gather to visit the graveyard en masse."

"How far to the border?" Brandon asked.

The man said it was about twenty miles. Isabel was in great shape, and so was he, but they couldn't walk that distance safely. The heat and humidity would slow them down, and they'd be out in the open for too long.

Isabel thanked the couple for the ride, exchanging pleasantries with the mother about her chubby baby, and Brandon handed the driver some cash for his trouble. They both waved as the small car sped away, leaving them near a popular hotel.

"We'll have to stay," she said. "At least for tonight."

"Yep."

She arched a brow at his clipped tone. "Would you rather see if we can rent bikes or something?"

He shoved his hands in his pockets, glancing at the darkening sky. It was late afternoon, and it smelled like rain. At this latitude, sudden showers were common. "Maybe tomorrow. Right now, we're stuck."

Her mouth tightened with displeasure. The money she'd saved was rapidly diminishing, but she wasn't going to ask him for anything. "I'll get us a room."

While she went inside Hotel del Camino, Brandon surveyed their surroundings, noting the bizarre holiday decorations. Posters depicting elegantly dressed skeletons graced most of the storefronts. A group of women were hanging wreaths of vibrant orange flowers on every lamppost. In addition to the roadblock signs, there was a large paper banner at the town's front entrance with rows of grinning skulls.

Although he knew he was in a surly mood, it seemed a little macabre—and devil-may-care—to throw a party for Death. What did the revelers do in the cemetery, dance on graves? Then again, he didn't have any room to judge. He'd lost his virginity to his high school girlfriend at the cemetery on Halloween night.

Isabel left the hotel with a piece of paper instead of a room key. "They're full because of the holidays. We can check elsewhere, but we might not find anything. The woman inside recommended a *casa de huespedes*."

"What's that?"

"A guesthouse or extra room offered by a host family," she said, showing him the printout, which was a simple map of the city. "This one is in a rural area, away from the center of town."

Brandon didn't like the idea of imposing on a family, but he wouldn't have felt comfortable in the hotel, either.

A remote or little-known location would be safer. And if they had limited privacy, he might survive the night.

They bought a few basic provisions at the market and grabbed some street food on the way out of town. Brandon could have eaten a dozen of the three-bite tacos Isabel purchased. The grilled fish tasted like it had jumped out of the ocean ten minutes ago, and the spicy red sauce drizzled over the top added a bright burst of flavor.

When he was finished with his to-go plate, he licked the sauce from his fingers and wished for more.

Isabel offered him fruit instead. She had a clear plastic bag filled with chopped melon. Without really thinking about it, he leaned forward, letting her pop a juicy slice into his mouth. As he chewed and swallowed the refreshing bite, she slid another piece of fruit between her lips, sucking gently.

Damned if that didn't remind him of something.

His cynical side suspected she was doing this on purpose. She had to know she'd driven him crazy on the bus earlier today. No straight guy on earth could watch a sexy woman lick a Popsicle without picturing himself in its place.

He forced himself to stop staring at her sweet-looking mouth and focus on the journey. "Where is this place?" he asked, eying the dark clouds overhead.

"The woman said a few miles."

They'd already walked at least three and the humidity was killing him. He felt irritable for a number of reasons. Sleep deprivation, sexual frustration, general anxiety. When thunder cracked in the sky, and the heavens opened up, his outlook didn't improve.

They were both soaked in minutes. Isabel began to shiver, but she didn't slow down or complain. Although his boots were weatherproof, her ratty canvas tennis shoes offered no protection from the rain. Or the pebble-strewn road, for that matter. If they had to cover several more miles, she'd get blisters.

"How are your feet?" he asked.

She gritted her teeth. "Fine."

The dirt road turned into wet mud, slippery and thick, adding another layer of difficulty. She slid sideways, almost losing her balance. He reached out to grip her wrist, steadying her. "Let me carry you."

"No," she said, jerking her arm from his grasp.

"You're going to get hurt."

"That's my problem."

"It's my problem, too, if you can't travel."

"Then you can just leave me!" she shouted, stomping forward.

Brandon stopped in his tracks, baffled by her outburst. Then he realized she was upset with him for switching gears so abruptly. In the car, he'd all but ground his erection against her. She'd expected him to be eager to bed her, not desperate to cross the border.

Cursing, because his hands were tied, he continued walking. He didn't care if she stayed angry, as long as she stayed with him. Maybe it was better this way, because he couldn't stand any more alluring glances.

Soon after, they came upon a sturdy-looking hacienda on a hill. She pointed to it, indicating that this was the place. There were several outbuildings, including what appeared to be a guest cabin.

They climbed the steps to the covered walkway, spirits lifting. A note was posted on the front door, written in Spanish.

"What does it say?" he asked.

As she scanned it, the hope drained from her face.

"The family is away for the holidays, so the guest quarters aren't available."

He swore bitterly, bracing his hands against the front door. Wanting to put his fist through it. Rain battered the adobe roof, pouring off the sides and rushing from the gutters. The temperature had dropped considerably, and although they weren't in danger of freezing this close to the equator, it would be a hard, cold night in wet clothes.

Isabel appeared ready to burst into tears. She took off her cap and furrowed a hand through her dark hair, which was plastered to her head. He knew at a glance that she couldn't continue walking in those useless shoes. The soles had probably been worn down on the sweltering road to Tehuantepec.

"I suppose you think this is my fault," she said hotly, following his gaze. "Like the long walk yesterday."

He sighed, shaking his head. He wasn't about to place blame on a woman who carried a dagger strapped to her thigh. As a fashion accessory, it looked sexy as hell. As a weapon, it was very effective.

"You should go on without me."

"Why would I do that?"

"You obviously can't wait to get to Guatemala."

"Because killers are after us, Isabel. Remember them?"

"They're after me, not you."

He shrugged, unconcerned with semantics.

"I don't need your protection," she said, her voice raw with emotion. "I don't want it! Just leave, okay? I have enough blood on my hands."

Her willingness to split up infuriated him. "You're such a damned martyr," he said, crowding her against the side of the house. "I'm not going anywhere."

She shoved at his chest. "Get away from me."

Although she was strong and determined, her efforts

failed to move him. They did incite him, however. He didn't like being pushed around, literally or figuratively. So he pushed back the only way he could without hurting her.

Gripping her chin in one hand, he lowered his mouth to hers.

Chapter 9

Isabel was prepared for a fight, not a sensual onslaught.

One moment they were involved a heated argument, the next he was silencing her with an insulting kiss. She didn't like it. She didn't like the firm grasp of his fingers, or the rough scrape of his beard stubble, or the careless way he plundered her mouth. She certainly didn't like him pinning her against the house, holding her prisoner.

Didn't he know she could pull her dagger and teach him a lesson?

She clenched her hands into fists, ready to pummel him. He wasn't making any attempt to secure her arms, but instead of striking him, she felt herself relax. Her body melted against his as he swept his tongue inside her mouth, penetrating her with bold strokes. He tasted like rain and heat and desperation. She moaned, threading her fingers through his hair and encouraging him to kiss *harder*.

Maybe she did like this.

With a low groan, he obliged her, plunging his tongue deep into her mouth. Her nipples puckered against the damp cups of her bra and need blossomed between her legs. Kissing him back with hungry bites, she explored the bunched muscles in his shoulders, digging her fingernails into his wet shirt.

He made a strangled sound and slid his hands to her bottom, cupping her soft flesh. She whimpered as he lifted her against him. When his erection slid along the cleft of her sex, creating an exquisite friction, she almost wept with pleasure.

Oh, God. She wanted that inside her. So bad.

Sitting on his lap earlier this afternoon had been torture. He'd felt like a thick, hot brand against her buttocks. She'd wanted to rub herself along that exciting length and bring his hands up to her taut nipples.

They'd both been aroused for hours.

His touch accessed that sweet agony, bypassing any slow build. Within seconds, they were panting, heaving, straining for more. He gripped her hips and tilted her for a better angle, as if seeking to penetrate her through their clothing. She gasped, wishing for no barriers between them as he thrust against her.

She was aware of the smell of rain and wet dirt, mingled with his earthy masculine scent. His skin felt cool beneath her fingertips, but they were generating so much heat that steam rose from his shoulders. Water rushed from the gutters in streaming rivulets and pounded the rooftop, urging them closer to the brink.

He released her, breathing heavily. "Let's break in."

She blinked at him, confused. He gestured toward the empty guest cabin in the distance, indicating that they seek shelter from the elements before continuing. Although she appreciated his thoughtfulness, she didn't need a bed. She was willing to do this against the door, in the mud, or under a tree.

"Come on," he said, dragging her away from the main house.

Rain pelted her hair and stung her hot cheeks, dampening her ardor. She almost expected Brandon to pick up a rock and smash through a window. That kind of action would have matched her urgency. When he proceeded to scan the perimeter of the small cabin with calm deliberation, she felt a surge of impatience.

It he didn't hurry up, she might come to her senses.

He found a narrow window which appeared to be unlocked, but it was no easy task to slide it open. Rain continued to pour on their heads as he went through a series of impromptu tools and unsuccessful strategies. He finally managed to inch the pane aside, creating a very narrow space to slip through.

"You'll fit," he said.

She let him boost her up, twisting her body to gain access. The window frame scraped her hip as she wriggled through, and there was nothing to break her fall on the way down. She sprawled across the tile floor, elbows and knees smarting.

"Are you okay?" Brandon asked, his voice muffled.

She squinted at the open window, torn between the urge to tell him off and the desire to finish what they'd started. Smothering a groan, she rose to her feet, studying her surroundings. A small, squeaky-looking brass bed dominated the room. She walked into the main area, which boasted a scarred wooden table with four chairs and a stone hearth.

No kitchen, no bathroom, no electricity. But beggars couldn't be choosers. Neither could wanted fugitives who were breaking and entering.

She unlocked the front door, letting him in.

"Damn" he said, smoothing a hand over his wet hair. "I thought you cracked your head open."

Shivering, she watched him check out the cozy space. He nodded his approval, apparently finding it secure and easy to defend. The cabin sat back on a hill, offering a clear view of the road. She wondered if he'd sleep tonight or stand guard.

When his gaze returned to her, wandering down the front of her body, she was once again aware of the hard points of her nipples against the wet fabric. The pale gray tank top and thin white bra were both soaked to transparency.

"I'll make a fire," he said, clearing his throat.

Next to the hearth, there was a box of wood. He found some matches and knelt down, snapping a few thin, dry branches for kindling.

Isabel realized that he wasn't raring to go anymore. *He* was the one who'd come to his senses. He'd broken in here to get dry and warm, not to bounce on the mattress with her. She should have appreciated his foresight. Instead, her stomach twisted with hurt. A few minutes ago, she'd been ready to strip naked for him in the rain. He must have felt something less powerful. A fleeting temptation, easily brushed aside.

The tears that had been threatening earlier sprang into her eyes. She turned on her heel and fled the room, horrified. Letting him see her cry was worse than throwing herself at him. She took a deep breath, struggling to hold the tears at bay.

Get it together, Isabel.

When her emotions calmed, she noticed a pair of light, multicolored blankets at the foot of the bed. She put one around her shoulders like a shawl, covering her exposed upper body. The other, she took to Brandon.

Maybe he was legitimately cold.

The fire was crackling in the main room, beginning to lick at the small logs he'd tossed in the hearth. He'd also removed his wet shirt, and didn't that add insult to injury? She'd seen bigger men, but none as well-proportioned. His lean muscles rippled in the firelight. He had a smattering of hair across his chest and more trailing down his etched stomach.

Before now, she'd have said that she preferred a smooth torso. But there was something so tantalizing about his rough-hewn flesh. One look at his raw, elemental male beauty converted her.

"Here," she said, throwing a blanket at him.

"Thanks." Sitting cross-legged in front of the fire, he draped it over his shoulders.

She settled in beside him, noting that he'd hung his shirt on the back of a chair to dry. She'd have to do the same if she wanted a dry outfit to wear tomorrow. Throwing her dirty garments into the flames sounded more appealing, however.

They stared at the flickering fire, saying nothing. Soon, the room began to warm, and her trembling subsided.

"You should get out of those wet clothes," he said.

She gave him an incredulous look. *Now* he wanted her clothes off?

He scrubbed a hand over his face, appearing tired and frustrated and at odds with himself.

"Look, I don't have any condoms. Do you?"

"No," she said, surprised. She'd assumed a man like him would be prepared.

"We can have a pretty good time without them, of course, but I think that would be tempting fate."

Her bitterness dissolved into a warm puddle of sexual images. Yes, she'd enjoy kissing and touching him all over, but what she wanted most was him inside her. And, after a long session of foreplay, she might beg for it.

He groaned, as if reading her thoughts. "I have other reasons, too."

"Like what?"

"The fact that you're on the run, for one."

She adjusted her blanket, uncomfortable.

"You also won't tell me why those men are after you, or what really happened."

"I can't talk about it," she said automatically, her shoulders stiffening. It was too difficult, too painful.

"If our situations were reversed, and I said I'd killed someone, would you feel safe enough to sleep with me?"

Her heart seized in her chest. He seemed to be suggesting that she was a threat to innocent people. "You think I'm dangerous?"

"I think you'd do anything to protect yourself," he said, his mouth hard.

She flushed with guilt, avoiding his gaze. Apparently, they were at an impasse. He didn't want to bed a psycho killer, and she couldn't defend her actions without giving him information that could be used against her.

"Do you want to keep living like this? Ducking and hiding?"

"You don't understand," she said, rising to her feet.

"Try me."

"My mother came looking for me once," she said, staring out the rain-spattered window. "I'd been calling her from a pay phone in downtown Tijuana. Not to talk, just to hear the sound of her voice. I was scared, and lonely."

"What happened?"

"I guess she knew it was me calling, because she

tracked down the location. She put up missing person posters and stood beside the pay phone for hours."

"Did you approach her?"

Isabel shook her head, bleak. "I couldn't. There was a man waiting in the alley the whole time. Watching her. He spotted me and gave chase."

"He didn't catch you?"

"No. I was lucky, because he was armed and I wasn't. I left Tijuana that night and started training, preparing for the next encounter."

"Why are you telling me this?"

"Because he could have killed her! If I'd let down my guard, and run to my mother, like I wanted to, he might have shot us both. Don't you see? Anyone close to me is at risk. Anyone who knows what I did is at risk."

"I can defend myself, Isabel. I can defend us both."

"What if they go after *your* family because you decided to play the hero? Can you live with that? Because I can't."

He came up behind her, grasping her upper arms. "I want to help you," he said, his mouth close to her ear. "Let me."

She shivered at his touch, her skin pebbling. But instead of leaning into his warm body, she shied away. "Don't. I shouldn't even be here with you. I can't give you what you want." And he couldn't give her what she wanted—damn him.

He raked a hand through his hair, sighing.

"Why don't you get some rest?" she said, her voice flat. "I'm not tired yet, and you only slept a few hours on the bus."

With a curt nod, he left the room, appearing as unsatisfied as she felt. She stared out the window for a long moment, trying not to let her emotions rule. Maybe it was better this way. The intensity of their attraction disturbed her, and she knew they couldn't have a real relationship. He was a tourist; she was a fugitive. Sooner or later, he would leave. It would be easier if she didn't get attached.

Darkness closed in and the rain let up. She fed the fire another log and glanced around the small room. There was a kerosene lamp on the table and a cast-iron cook pot near the hearth. She'd kill for a hot bath. She couldn't remember the last time she'd soaked in a tub. That wasn't going to happen, but she could wash her face, at least, and rinse out her clothes before she hung them up to dry.

She slipped out the front door and did a visual search of the grounds, looking for a hose or water spigot. A quaint little structure on the hillside caught her eye. A well—of course. There was a sturdy plastic bucket beside the door. She picked it up, moving quickly in the fading evening light. Rainwater dripped from the eaves and tree branches, splashing her face. Filling the bucket wasn't a difficult task, but it took time and effort. She transferred the first gallon to the cook pot and went back for one more.

Brandon didn't complain about the minor commotion she was making. Perhaps he guessed what she was doing. The mattress springs creaked under his weight but he didn't get up. She locked the front door as a precaution and put the pot over the fire. While she was waiting for the water to heat, she found some string and fashioned a simple clothesline.

The cabin wasn't devoid of all amenities. There was a small crate in the corner with strips of linen and a bar of soap inside. She sat down on the rug in front of the fire, rubbing her bare arms. Soon, steam rose from the water, and the room glowed with warmth. She removed the pot from the fire and dipped the linen inside, testing the temperature. It was perfect. Tugging off her wet clothes, she took a leisurely sponge bath, dragging the rough fabric over her naked limbs.

Although she was aware that Brandon could walk in at any moment, she didn't rush. Maybe he was listening to the soft splash of water, picturing her like this. She wanted him to want her. To ache like she ached.

It took every ounce of willpower she possessed to set aside the linen washcloth. Her nipples jutted forward, begging for more stimulation. Between her legs, she was moist and swollen. The temptation to touch herself was overwhelming.

Flushing, she wrapped a blanket around her wet body and tossed her clothes into the soapy water. After giving them a good scrub, she rinsed the garments, wrung them out as best she could and hung them up to dry.

Brandon's clothes needed washing, too. She listened for the sound of bedsprings but heard only his deep breathing. So much for him lying awake, pining for her. On tiptoe, she sneaked into the bedroom and grabbed his cargo pants from the floor.

He reached out and locked his hand around her wrist, fast as lightning.

"You don't want me to wash these?" she asked, her heart pounding.

With a low groan, he let go of her, rolling over in bed. His response was muffled, incoherent. She wasn't sure he'd actually woken up. Unsettled by his quick reflexes, she took the pants with her, along with his socks and boxer shorts.

When the washing was finished, she curled up in front of the fire with the thin blanket, using a folded towel as a pillow. If she climbed into bed with Brandon, he'd probably get up to stand guard. She didn't think Carranza's men would be searching remote cabins near the Guatemalan border in the middle of the night, however. With-out a good four-wheel drive vehicle, they'd have trouble getting here during the day.

For now, she felt safe.

She also felt restless, despite her fatigue. Flames danced in the hearth, warming the small space, inviting her to bare all. She wanted to be naked here, in front of the fire.

If she had a little more nerve, she'd let the blanket fall off her shoulders, exposing her bare breasts. She would cup her tender flesh and toy with her stiff nipples, pinch-ing them gently. When she was ready, she would smooth her hand down her belly and part her trembling thighs, stroking herself to climax.

The possibility of getting caught made the fantasy twice as hot. Would Brandon enjoy watching her?

Although she longed for release, and a blissful sleep, she wouldn't be satisfied with her own soft touch. She wanted his rough handling, his callused fingers and ag-gressive mouth. She wanted his firm grip, holding her wrists over her head. His hard chest against her breasts. His thick length, filling every inch of her.

But she couldn't have that. She couldn't have any of that.

Eyes glittering with unshed tears, she rolled away from the fire. Naked, and alone, and emptier than ever.

When Isabel fell silent, Brandon breathed a sigh of relief, stifling the urge to grind his erection against the mattress.

He'd listened to her bathe, his ears straining for every sound, imagination running wild. He wanted to hear her soft panting and sweet little gasps of pleasure. He wanted her sobbing with ecstasy, shuddering beneath him.

That was impossible, so he tortured himself with solo

fantasies. Although he doubted she was masturbating quietly, less than ten feet away from him, he couldn't stop thinking about it. The idea of her touching her pretty breasts, or fingering her slick, hot sex while she moaned his name, drove him over the edge.

He wanted her so damned bad.

Closing his eyes, he focused on controlling his breathing. His stiff arousal surged against the sheets, threatening to erupt. Kissing her had been a mistake. He wished he could erase the feel of her body and the taste of her mouth.

Now he knew how good it would be between them.

He forced himself to relax, calm down and consider his objective. Trust and integrity were huge in his line of work. He couldn't throw his career away for one hot night. Getting romantically involved with a target was against the rules.

She'd also be devastated when she found out who he really was. Sleeping with her under false pretenses was like...sexual warfare. It wasn't moral, or ethical, or decent. He didn't lie to women to get them in bed.

He couldn't have her. Bottom line.

Normally he collected information that could be used against the target. Circumstantial evidence, background history, criminal connections. With Isabel, he'd started doing the opposite. He wanted to help exonerate her.

Maybe if he cleared her name, they could meet again, start over. But it was far more likely that she'd hate him forever.

Gritting his teeth, he punched the pillow under his head. No matter what, he was destined to do wrong by her.

He was contractually obligated to betray her.

When his blood had cooled, and the only sound coming from the main room was that of the crackling logs, he rose from the bed. Securing the blanket around his waist, he walked through the open doorway. Isabel was curled up on the floor, her hands tucked beneath her head, hair spilling across her bare shoulders.

Their wet clothes hung on a string-line near the hearth, her panties next to his shorts. He'd never had a live-in girlfriend, and couldn't recall a woman ever washing his clothes before. He wasn't sure how he felt about it.

Luckily, he'd transferred the important documents from his cargo pants to a hidden compartment in his backpack.

Isabel didn't wake when he knelt before her, scooping her off the ground. She was heavier than he'd figured, and her sleeping form made an unwieldy bundle. He could smell her hair and feel the silken heat of her skin as he carried her toward the bedroom. Hoping she wouldn't rouse, he placed her on the mattress as gingerly as possible.

He wanted to strip away the blanket and eat her with his eyes. But it was dark in the room, and he'd only just gained mastery over his desire. Studying her nude body while she slept was also an invasion of privacy.

Clenching his jaw, he covered her with the bedsheets and walked away.

After checking the lock and doing a final sweep of the premises, he settled down in the space she'd just inhabited. He didn't toss another log on, as the room was warm enough and smoke gave away their presence. It wasn't a big concern because most houses in Tapachula had cooking fires, but it didn't hurt to be careful.

There was a damp washcloth hanging over the plastic bucket. On impulse, he brought the fabric to his nose and inhaled. It smelled like mild soap and cool water and Isabel. Longing welled up inside him, from a deeper place than lust. Wrapping the cloth around his fist, he pressed his lips to it, staring at the glowing embers until sleep overtook him.

Chapter 10

Isabel awoke to a strange sound.

Opening her eyes, she realized that she was alone in the bedroom. The room was bright with early-morning light. Sitting up in bed, she clutched the sheet to her chest, listening for another sharp crack.

It came, preceded by a faint hissing sound.

The striped blanket she'd been using as a toga was tangled around her ankles. She wrapped it around her body and walked to the window, curious. Brandon was outside, stripped to the waist, chopping wood. The cargo pants she'd washed last night rode low on his hips and his chest glistened with perspiration. While she watched, he drew back the ax and let it sing through the air, splitting a thick log.

She backed away from the window, her throat dry. It wasn't fair for a man to be so relentlessly good-looking. Shivering, she walked into the main room. The fire had burned down to ash, and he'd replaced the wash water with a fresh bucket. Noticing the ladle hanging by the hearth, she dipped it into the bucket, getting herself a cool drink.

The clothes on the line were still damp. They'd probably dry faster in the sun, now that the rain had passed. With a small sigh, she grabbed her messenger bag and returned to the bedroom for a quick morning toilette. There she noticed a small pine chest at the foot of the bed. She hadn't seen it yesterday.

Opening the lid, she found a threadbare quilt, a few candles and a Spanish-language Bible. Under the quilt, she hit the jackpot: a pair of huarache sandals and an embroidered tunic. Eyes widening, she brought out the traditional garment, called a *huipil.* It was turquoise with dark blue flowers, and quite beautiful.

Letting the blanket drop, she donned the colorful tunic, which cinched in at the waist and covered her to midthigh. It was supposed to be worn with a long skirt, but she could pair it with pants once hers were dry. Smiling, she tried on the soft leather sandals. Like the *huipil,* they were only a little too large.

She fashioned her hair into two braids and strapped her dagger to her thigh, delighted by her new duds. A few years ago, she wouldn't have felt this good wearing a designer dress and expensive heels.

Brandon stopped chopping wood as soon as she came outside. He did a double take, his gaze lingering on her bare legs. She was acutely aware of her nudity beneath the tunic. "Wow. You look like an Aztec princess."

She blushed, shaking her head. "I'm not even Mexican."

"You could pass, in that outfit."

"I suppose you could call me a *mestizo,*" she said, using the word for mixed race. "My mother is South American."

He nodded, resuming his task. There was more tension between them now, along with an unspoken agreement to avoid intimacy. He must have carried her to the bedroom last night, choosing once again to take on the role of guardian. A part of her hoped he'd slept, but she also entertained a vindictive wish that he'd stayed up, aching for her.

She made use of the outhouse and strolled the grounds of the small farm. There was an empty goat pen and a full chicken coop. She picked up the basket by the door and ventured inside, collecting a half-dozen eggs. Emerging triumphant, she marveled at her station in life. She'd really gone country.

"What are you going to do with those?" Brandon asked.

"Boil them. Are you hungry?"

"Starving."

She built up the fire a little and put water on to heat, rummaging through the goods they'd bought at the market. Soon they had a light breakfast of hard-boiled eggs, goat cheese and warm tortillas. Brandon seemed to appreciate the meal, even though it was meatless. They could have beef jerky and fresh fruit for lunch.

Before sitting down to eat, he'd washed up and put on a shirt. The bruise under his eye had faded into a faint smudge, and the cut above appeared to be healing well. "What happened to your bandage?" she asked.

"It fell off."

Finishing her last bite of tortilla, she grabbed the first aid kit from her bag. Although he insisted he didn't need it, she dabbed a bit of antibiotic ointment on the wound and applied a smaller bandage.

After breakfast, she transferred the clothesline to a sunny spot outside, and he covered their tracks by dousing the fire. He also replaced the wood they'd burned and stacked more in neat piles. His hard work was a payment for their stay. She did her part, making the bed and tidying up the place while he kept his eye on the road.

"Do you want to try to walk?" she asked, feeling uneasy. It was frustrating to be stuck here, mere miles from Guatemala, at a sexual stalemate.

"I doubt we could make it by nightfall."

"What about bikes? Or another motorcycle?"

"Assuming we could find either kind of transportation for a decent price, we'd still be on the road alone, exposed."

She nodded in agreement. Her funds were already low, and they probably couldn't rent bikes on a holiday.

"It would be less risky to wait for a bus or an opportunity to hitchhike tomorrow." Remembering her map of the city, she retrieved the square of paper from her bag and spread it out on the table. "Here's the bus station," she said, tapping her finger on it. Other local landmarks were represented, along with a few businesses. The parade route was highlighted in orange. It started at the graveyard and proceeded through the center of town. "The cemetery is just over this hill," she said, pointing to an area behind the hacienda. "A crowd will be gathered there most of the day."

"To do what?"

"Decorate the grave sites. If I remember correctly, they make offerings to the dead. Favorite foods and drinks."

He arched a brow. "Do they eat it?"

She smiled, shaking her head. "I don't know. I think it's more symbolic."

"Let's go check it out."

"Really?" she said, surprised.

"Sure," he said with a shrug. "It's only a few miles, and we can stay off the main roads. I saw a trail out back."

"The goat trail." She'd seen the narrow dirt path, too. "Maybe it's a shortcut."

Anything was better than staying inside the cramped cabin, trying to ignore the tension between them. She couldn't pretend her desire didn't exist; it was obvious in every furtive glance she gave him.

Isabel got ready to leave, grabbing her still-damp pants from the clothesline and putting them on under her tunic. She also folded the blanket she'd used and replaced it in the crate. Everything else she left hanging, hoping it would dry by the time they returned. The only item she couldn't find was the strip of linen she'd used as a washcloth.

Brandon brought his backpack, which held bottled water and a picnic lunch, among other things. He had the gun on him, which bothered her. She'd chosen to train with a knife because it was less deadly. Her intention had been to defend herself, not endanger human lives. On that front, she'd failed, and failed, and failed.

They took off toward the rolling hills, the sun peeking through the clouds. It was a warm, humid day, but not unpleasant. Isabel had grown accustomed to the tropical climate and bore it better than Brandon, who perspired in a manly, endearing sort of way.

"Damn," he said, wiping his forehead. "You look like a hothouse flower and I'm dripping with sweat."

She waved off the compliment, and his concerns, conjuring a detailed image of him chopping wood. "I like sweat."

"Do you have a stinky sock fetish, too?"

"No," she said, laughing.

"In that case, thanks for washing my clothes."

"You're welcome."

They fell into a charged silence, saving their energy

for the climb. She felt self-conscious about her domestic behavior and wondered if it seemed desperate. Her dad's groupies were like that, needy and overeager. At every concert, thousands of manic, half-naked women had screamed his name.

She'd never understood why he'd loved them more than her.

The hills gave way to a lush green valley, where the air was cooler. Birds chirped and spider monkeys chattered in the trees, as if excited about the festivities. At the base of the valley there was a large cemetery. A crowd had gathered, leaving a trail of marigold petals in their wake, and vendors had set up stands to sell a variety of goods.

Brandon and Isabel paused, surveying the scene from a distance. It looked like a county fair at a graveyard. "What's that orange stuff for?"

"The flower petals lead the dead home for a short visit."

He shifted the weight of his backpack, his expression dubious. "This is an odd holiday."

Isabel smiled and shrugged, agreeing that the celebration had quirky elements. But it was also reverent and meaningful, despite the gaiety. "It's just their way of honoring loved ones who've passed away."

They didn't see any of Carranza's men, hoping to send *them* to the underworld, so they continued down into the valley. The day was sunny and bright, and the colorful decorations created a happy chaos. Hundreds of noisy revelers made it simple to blend in and disappear. They were probably safer here than at the cabin.

For the first hour, they walked through the busy cemetery, studying the decorated grave sites. Many were adorned with handpicked flowers, letters from family members and children's crafts. Others were laden with food and drink.

"This guy's ready to party," Brandon said, gesturing to a six pack of Modelo resting against a headstone.

She laughed, twining her arm through his. They must have passed dozens of shot glasses, but she hadn't felt tempted to partake. Perhaps all of her longing was wrapped up in him. When her gaze moved to the next site over, her humor evaporated.

Many of the graves had no markers; simple wooden crosses were common. This one had an engraved headstone that read *Nuestra Bebe*. A pair of tiny pink booties had been placed on the grassy mound.

"Oh," she breathed, covering her mouth with one hand.

He pulled her closer, hugging her head to his chest. After a quiet moment, they continued toward the front entrance, their footsteps a little heavier. Outside the gate, vendors were selling marigold bouquets, fresh-baked bread and glass-encased candles. There was a communal altar set up for *almas perdidas*.

"What does that mean?" Brandon asked, glancing at the sign above the altar.

"Lost souls," Isabel translated. "It's a place to pay tribute to loved ones who are missing or buried elsewhere."

He took a few dollars out of his pocket, approaching the candle vendor. "Do you want one?"

"Why not?" she murmured, her stomach churning.

He chose a white candle and she picked a purple one. Together, they walked toward the altar, placing the candles side by side. He lit both with a long match from the table. Isabel supposed it was customary to recite a short prayer when making an offering, but she didn't know what to say. She stared at the flame until her eyes watered.

Brandon didn't speak, either. He glanced skyward in silent contemplation and then looked at her, gauging her reaction. When another woman came to the altar to light her candle, they stepped aside.

He bought a sample of *pan de muerto,* placing the sweet bread in his backpack. "Are you ready to have our picnic?"

Although she wasn't hungry, she said yes. They left the graveyard the same way they came, via goat path, and found a shady tree on a gentle slope to spread out the quilt she'd brought. Sitting down together, they drank cool water, admiring the view. There were lush green hills as far as the eye could see.

"Who was your candle for?" she asked, curious.

He stretched out with his hands behind his head, looking up at the arching tree branches. "A buddy of mine."

She studied his face. "How close?"

"One of my best friends. We grew up together."

"How did he die?"

"Combat fire in Iraq. Earlier this year."

"I'm sorry," she said.

"Are you?"

"Of course," she said, shame coloring her cheeks. None of her friends had died fighting for their country. Most of her acquaintances had been too busy wasting their own lives to worry about saving others. "That's awful."

He stared back at her for a moment, pensive. "We were supposed to take a surfing trip as soon as his tour ended."

"Is that why you came alone?"

"I think so. I couldn't bear to replace him."

"Do you ever feel guilty?" she asked, her heart pounding with anxiety. "For being alive, I mean?"

"No," he said quietly. "I feel guilty for not going. We both talked about enlisting but he was the only one who followed through."

She ran her palm over the blades of grass beside the blanket, feeling the soft prickle.

"Who was your candle for?" he asked.

"My dad."

"What did he die of?"

"Nothing heroic," she said with a bitter smile.

"Tell me about it."

She stared out into the distance, unsure where to start. "I told you that he got remarried, right?"

"Right."

"My mom got remarried, too, when I was fourteen. I resented my dad for never visiting and made no effort to get along with my stepdad. I started skipping school to surf, experimenting with drugs. And boys."

His brows rose. "How did that go over?"

"Not well. By the time I turned sixteen, I was totally out of control. My mom didn't know what to do with me. She finally sent me to my dad's."

"Is that what you wanted?"

"I thought it was," she said, plucking a blade of grass and twisting it around her finger. "He had a different lifestyle. Late-night parties and jet-setting. Even when he was there, he wasn't really *there*. And I entered the picture at the worst possible time."

"Why?"

"His second marriage was already on the rocks. He was battling addiction and she begged him to go to rehab. The only thing I cared about was surfing, and getting high, so my presence created more problems. Right before I graduated I got kicked out of school. They argued about it, and he went on a drug binge. She left him."

"You feel responsible?"

She bent the blade of grass in two. "Yes. We didn't see each other much after that. I moved into my own apartment and did my own thing. A few years later, he drove his Ferrari off the side of a cliff. Drunk and stoned."

He didn't ask if she felt responsible for that, as well. Perhaps it was obvious. "Were you angry?"

"Yes," she said, surprised by his intuition, "but I couldn't find a way to express it. Everyone spoke highly of him at the funeral, as if he was some kind of god. He'd touched so many people's lives, but never bothered to be a part of mine."

"His mistake."

She blinked the tears from her eyes, taking a deep breath. "I don't remember much of the following year. I was a mess. You'd think his death would have scared me straight, but no. I masked the pain with pills and parties."

He waited for her to continue, his attention rapt.

"My mom tried to help me, but I refused to see her," she said, dusting the grass bits from her hands. She wanted to stop there, but the words tumbled forth, spilling from her lips. "That's when I met Jaime. Manuel Carranza's son." As the head of La Familia, Carranza was infamous. Brandon knew she was sharing a dangerous tale, and he understood the consequences of hearing it.

"Go on," he said, ready for the rest of the story.

"I didn't know who his father was at the time. I just thought he was a handsome rich boy with a lot of dope. We hooked up one night and went back to my apartment. I'm not sure what we did there, besides more drugs."

"Did he try to hurt you?" Brandon asked.

"No," she said, swallowing a nervous laugh. "God no. We were too high to function. He'd never been interested in me, sexually. When I woke up the next day he was dead beside me, and my bottle of pills was empty."

"You gave them to him?"

"I have no idea. I panicked, grabbed everything I could think of. His stuff, my stuff. And then I just left. Drove across the border, looking for another escape. Later, I saw a news report about his family connections."

"Why did you say you owed money to the cartel?"

"Because I took Jaime's kit with me. It was full of cash, and drugs. I went through both in less than a month."

He shook his head. "Wow."

"Yeah. When I ran out, I didn't know what to do. I couldn't use my credit cards or go to the bank. I had no resources, no survival skills, no friends to speak of."

At one point, she'd tried to get a modeling job, although she was terrified of being recognized. The talent agent said she was too thin, by Mexico's standards. Too thin to model. "I ended up at the Red Light district."

He flinched at the admission, uncomfortable. She felt a tiny pinprick of satisfaction, along with a wave of shame. At last, she'd managed to shock him. He might not blame her for being an addict, but he found fault with her whoring.

"I got picked up right away."

A muscle in his jaw flexed. "Of course you did."

"The guy was handsome, wealthy and about my father's age. He took me to a nice hotel, and he was very kind."

"I don't want to hear this."

But she had to say it. The memory was like a black stain on her heart, eating it from the inside out. Maybe if she told him the ugly truth, she could feel clean again. "When he asked me to undress, I burst into tears. I think he felt sorry for me, because he didn't force anything. He left some money and his business card, saying he could set me up in an apartment. He knew I didn't belong on the street."

Brandon raked a hand through his hair, swearing.

"I stayed in the hotel, staring at the money crumpled in

my fist. There was a pharmacy around the corner where I could buy pills. I thought about it for a long time."

"Why didn't you do it?"

"How do you know I didn't?"

"Because you're here with me, instead of in some rich asshole's apartment."

She brought her knees up and wrapped her arms around them, making herself small. "There was a radio in the hotel room. He'd turned it on to calm me down, I guess. They get San Diego stations in Tijuana. It was 91X, I think. This song by Everclear came on. 'Father of Mine.' Do you know that one?"

"Yes," he said, his voice hoarse.

"I'd heard it before but never paid much attention to the lyrics. For some reason, I stopped and listened. It's about a man thinking back on his childhood, wondering why his father abandoned him. It's an angry song. Emotional."

"Right."

Her throat tightened and the tears built behind her eyes, demanding release. "I hadn't really been sober since the funeral, so I hadn't grieved. All of these feelings came to the surface when I heard the song. I must have cried for hours, but it wasn't for him. It was for me." She brought a fist to the center of her chest, where she ached. "He didn't deserve my love. He was a bad father, and it was okay for me to be angry."

Brandon put his arm around her, drawing her close. For a few minutes, he stroked her hair while she pressed her face to his shirt.

"I left the hotel and got clean, all on my own. I started surfing again. The incident with my mom happened soon after." She choked out the next words, tears seeping from her eyes. "I have so many regrets, but the worst of them is pushing her away before I left. And my biggest fear is that I'll never see her again."

"Shh," he said, kissing the top of her head. "You'll see her."

His calm assurance comforted her like nothing else ever had. She wanted to believe him, to trust in him. She'd also figured out what she had to do as soon as they crossed the border into Guatemala, and coming to the decision wasn't easy.

It would be a shame to leave him without ever having *had* him. She tilted her face up to his, wishing for something to remember him by. He cupped her cheek, brushing away the tears with his thumb. Pulse racing, she moistened her trembling lips.

They were alone on the hillside, protected by shade, away from prying eyes. His gaze swept the immediate area and returned to her mouth, darkening with desire. She could feel his heart beating against hers, strong and sure.

"I shouldn't do this," he said, and bent his head to kiss her.

Chapter 11

Brandon couldn't help himself.

He knew it was wrong for him to take advantage of a vulnerable woman, but she was just so lovely like this. Her eyelashes were wet with tears, her mouth soft and uncertain. She'd just told him her darkest secret, her deepest shame and biggest fear. The least he could do was comfort her. Kiss it better.

But the instant his lips touched hers, she shied away from him. "It bothered you, the idea of me...selling myself?"

"Yes."

She closed her eyes, more tears sliding down her cheeks. "Then you should know that there have been other men, other hotel rooms. Not all of them were like Jaime."

"What do you mean?"

"Some were more than friends. And I didn't always say no."

"Did they always listen when you did?"

She nodded.

His shoulders, which had tensed at her words, relaxed. "I've been in my share of hotel rooms, Isabel. And I've had plenty of casual girlfriends."

"Why don't you have one now?"

He stretched out on his back again, letting her snuggle into the crook of his arm. "I don't know. I travel a lot."

"Do you have a different woman in every city?"

"No," he said, swallowing a laugh. He could see that she'd posed the question seriously, as if she thought he was that type of guy. Maybe he used to be. "I just haven't dated anyone lately. Right before my buddy was killed in Iraq, another friend of mine went through a difficult divorce. He'd married young and hadn't really played the field. I guess he felt like living it up. He started drinking heavily, going out to clubs."

She toyed with a button on his shirt. "Did you go with him?"

"Once or twice. But I didn't enjoy myself."

"Why not?"

He shrugged, trying to pinpoint a reason. "I think I'd outgrown it. I'd had enough drunken hookups in college. There was also something sleazy about my friend's attitude, like he wanted to sleep with as many women as possible to get back at his ex."

Her gaze rose from his shirtfront. "How old are you?"

"Twenty-seven. You?"

"Twenty-three."

He knew that already, of course, and regretted having to pretend otherwise.

"So you haven't dated since your friend died," she said, studying him. "And you lost interest in casual relationships."

Heat crept up his neck, as if she'd accused him of losing interest in sex. That was hardly the case, as evidenced by his body's constant state of arousal in her presence. "I didn't want to waste my time unless I met someone special."

As soon as the words left his mouth, he wished he could take them back. Not because she wasn't special—she was—but because encouraging this level of intimacy would make his betrayal cut even deeper.

Too late. Her eyes rounded with understanding, then darkened with desire. She lifted her head from his bicep, flattening her palm on his chest. He tried to ignore the feel of her slender fingers through the thin fabric, the sultry heat in her expression. But when she slid her thigh along his and pressed her lips to the hollow of his throat, he couldn't control his reaction. The blood rushed from his head to his groin, swelling him to a painful fullness. She licked him like a kitten, lapping at a cord in his neck.

With a strangled growl, he grasped one of her braids and pulled her head up, aligning her mouth to his. She parted her lips eagerly, threading her fingers through his short hair. He tasted the salt of his skin on her tongue.

Because she was half-sprawled over him, her knee dangerously close to his erection, Brandon couldn't control the kiss. She clutched his hair and squirmed against him, encouraging him to fill her mouth. He plunged his tongue deep, giving her what she asked for, wanting to give her a whole lot more. Fighting the urge to roll her onto her back, he moved his hands down to her lush little bottom, cupping her soft flesh. She wasn't wearing panties. Groaning, he moved beneath the drawstring waistline, palming her bare backside.

Her skin felt like hot silk.

She gasped and shifted her weight on him, fitting his

straining erection against the apex of her thighs. When she released her grip on his hair and started fumbling with the buttons at his shirtfront, he knew he was in trouble.

Soon, she'd be nibbling her way down his chest.

Hoping to distract her, he took his hands out of her pants and put them inside her top. She wasn't wearing a bra, but he'd known that already. Her nipples were clearly defined beneath the Spanish-style blouse, striking a sharp contrast between demure and erotic. He covered her sleek curves with his hands, reverent.

She sat up to give him easier access, straddling his hips. Watching her face intently, he brushed his thumb over one pouty nipple, then the other. Her eyes glittered with arousal and her cheeks were passion-flushed.

"I want to see you," he said, moistening his lips.

She glanced around the deserted hillside, making sure they were alone. After a brief hesitation, she pulled her shirt over her head, exposing her breasts. They were small and exquisite, topped with dusky little nipples.

"You're so beautiful," he said in a hoarse voice, skimming her slender rib cage, framing her breasts with his hands. He pinched her nipples between his thumb and forefinger, applying gentle pressure. She groaned, rubbing her hot cleft against his swollen erection. He was painfully hard.

She whimpered, moving faster. He undid the drawstring at her waist and watched her pants settle lower on her hips. She looked so sexy on top of him, her stomach bare and her breasts free. He wanted to make her come. Sliding the flat of his hand down her belly, he found her slick center. She was hot, slippery, delicious. Entranced, he brought his mouth to her nipple, flicking his tongue over the tight bead. At the same time, he stroked the taut nub at the crest of her sex, strumming his fingertips back and forth.

Then her body stiffened, and not with pleasure. "Oh!" she exclaimed, scrambling off him.

He had his gun out of his backpack before he rolled over. In the next instant, he was aiming at a flash of movement along the path. The stray goat looked as startled as they were. It burst into a fast trot, disappearing over the hill.

Brandon glanced at Isabel, whose shoulders were shaking with mirth. He engaged the safety and put his gun away, feeling foolish. She righted her clothes and curled up next to him on the blanket, covering her face with her hands.

"Is public sex frowned on in Mexico?" he asked.

She dissolved in giggles.

"I guess we're lucky that goat didn't have an owner with him."

"Yes," she said, wiping her eyes.

The sensual interlude was over, but desire still hummed between them like an electric undercurrent. "After we cross the border, will you come to the U.S. embassy with me? Maybe we can talk to the police, get some information about your case."

Her smile faded, replaced by fear and tension. She looked away, uncertain.

"I'm worried about you," he said, cupping her chin. "I'm afraid you'll disappear and I'll never see you again."

She met his gaze, her face quiet, full of sorrow.

Again, he was taking a huge professional risk. Encouraging a target to surrender was so far out-of-bounds that he almost couldn't believe he was doing it. But, if she went willingly into custody, she might escape with a lighter punishment.

"I'll think about it and let you know," she said.

His heart swelled with hope. Stupid, horny, inappropriate hope. He squelched it, knowing there was no future for them. They only had this time, this place. And he wasn't strong enough to deny himself the pleasure of her body in the interim.

Leaning forward, he kissed the corner of her mouth. "I want to touch you," he said, moving his lips close to her ear. "Back at the cabin, where you can take off your clothes. I want to taste you." He couldn't enter her without a condom, but he'd love to satisfy her with his hands and mouth. Excited by the thought, he drew her earlobe into his mouth and sucked gently, worrying the tender flesh with his tongue.

She inhaled a ragged breath and he released her with a low groan. The minute they got behind closed doors, he was going to throw her down on that squeaky bed, strip her naked and lick every inch of that sweet little body.

Dwelling on that fantasy would make walking difficult, so he drove it from his mind, helping her fold the quilt they'd been picnicking on. They hadn't eaten much, but he wasn't hungry for food. As they descended the hillside, he tried to focus on the story she'd told him. Every detail was important to her case.

The death investigation for Jaime Carranza had been kept open for several reasons. Toxicology results revealed he'd overdosed on a dangerous mixture of pills, alcohol and street drugs. Normally, that wouldn't arouse suspicion, but his family had a lot of enemies, increasing the chances of foul play. Isabel had also fled the scene, taking the evidence, and Jaime's belongings, with her. Brandon knew that the strongest pills had come from her prescription bottle; several stray capsules had been found in his mouth. Jaime had either lost consciousness in the process of swallowing, or someone had force-fed the pills to him. He doubted Isabel was responsible.

Robbery was a common motive in drug-related homicide, and the fact that Isabel left a dead body in her home without calling police was problematic. Even if she hadn't meant to hurt him, which Brandon firmly believed, she could face a stiff punishment. And after he turned her in, her fate was out of his hands.

If she came to harm he'd never forgive himself.

Frowning at the thought, he considered another troublesome inconsistency. Jaime had been a ladies' man. He was rarely seen without female company and often entertained an entourage of party girls. But, according to Isabel, they were just friends and he'd never made a pass. That struck Brandon as odd. Had drugs obliterated Jaime's libido so much that he wasn't interested in sex?

Brandon couldn't imagine a man not wanting Isabel in his bed.

They made their way toward the hacienda, his mind in turmoil. Maybe he should be helping Isabel escape, rather than plotting her capture. What if she'd be better off in Central America than the U.S.? He pictured them living in a quaint cottage on the beach, surfing all day, enjoying a life of idyllic perfection. Isabel would wear flowers in her hair. He'd grow a beard. They'd watch the sunset together.

He shook his head, dispelling the dreamy images. If he stayed with Isabel, he'd never see his parents again. There was nothing idyllic about being on the run. And he certainly wasn't ready to retire.

As they traversed the final stretch of path, the hairs on the nape of his neck prickled with unease. Something was amiss. "Wait," he murmured, gesturing for Isabel to crouch with him behind the stone well. Cursing, he drew his weapon.

They'd been found.

Isabel followed his gaze, seeing the fresh tire tracks in front of the house.

The vehicle appeared to have backed out and turned around. The telltale grooves veered into a copse of trees a few hundred yards down the road. A black SUV was parked in the shade, almost hidden.

She gasped, ducking down lower. "Have they spotted us?"

"I can't tell," he answered.

The SUV was lying in ambush, as if its inhabitants expected them to come out of the cabin. Carranza's men might not have noticed their approach. It was late afternoon now, and long shadows cloaked the hillside.

"Maybe they'll go away."

"No. They'll wait."

Knowing this was true, she clenched her hand into a tight fist. The clothesline she'd put up made it obvious that they planned to return. She shouldn't have left any hint of their presence. "I'm sorry."

"Don't be."

"I didn't think they'd find us all the way out here."

"Me, either," he admitted.

Pulse pounding with fear, she considered the clues they'd left along the way. If the taxi they'd ditched had turned up on the side of a road, halfway to Guatemala, the men would know where they were headed. It was also possible that they'd spoken to the checkpoint soldiers or bribed the Tapachula locals.

"At dusk, we'll make a run for it," he said. "Go back to the graveyard."

She braced her shoulders on the stone wall and took a deep breath. "The parade goes straight down the main drag. Maybe we can disappear in the crowd."

He nodded, keeping his eyes on the SUV. "We'll leave as soon as it's dark."

As it happened, they didn't have to wait. The SUV pulled out of its hiding place, heading right at them.

"Go," Brandon shouted, shoving her toward the goat path.

She scrambled up the hill, her heart in her throat. Shots rang out, hissing through the air and furrowing into the grass near her feet. Brandon didn't stop to return fire. Keeping his body between her and the approaching vehicle, he pushed her to climb faster.

The SUV couldn't find purchase on the steep incline. It stalled, engine roaring, wheels churning in the soft earth.

Isabel registered these sounds as they sailed over the top of the hill. Brandon jerked her to the ground, flattening his body on top of hers. For a breath-stealing moment, he aimed his gun at the vehicle, trading shots with Carranza's men.

She held her hands over her ears, terrified. Bullets peppered the hillside, raining loose dirt on their heads.

"I'm out," he said, swearing as he ejected the clip. Within seconds, he'd located spare ammunition and reloaded.

She didn't have time to wonder where the extra round had come from, because he pulled her to her feet and they started running again. No gunshots dogged their steps as they raced down the path. At the base of the next hill, they stopped again, taking shelter behind a large tree. "Are you hit?" he asked, skimming her body for injuries.

"No, I'm fine. Are they?"

"I don't know. I shattered the front windshield."

The engine revved up, proving that someone was alive inside. The noise faded into the distance as the SUV drove away.

"Come on," he said, urging her to keep moving. "The passenger might follow us on foot. We can't afford to let him catch up."

She picked up the pace, struggling to match his stride. They couldn't risk waiting to ambush their pursuer, and hiding out in the open woods wasn't safe. The best choice was to stay on course and hope they arrived at the cemetery first.

"With the roads closed, he'll have to ditch the SUV somewhere," Brandon pointed out. "We can beat them."

Summoning endurance, she redoubled her efforts, sprinting along the narrow dirt path. Her muscles burned from exertion but fatigue wasn't her greatest obstacle. The soft leather sandals she wore fit loose, and they weren't built for speed. The ankle straps rubbed at every stress point, cutting into her skin.

The foot pain was minor compared to the hitch in her chest. She realized that she couldn't go on like this. Although she'd planned to slip away from Brandon after they crossed the border, now she knew she couldn't wait.

Their chances of survival were slim. Carranza's men had found them. They'd shot at Brandon repeatedly, going for the kill. They might keep her alive for questioning, but they needed nothing from him.

Earlier this afternoon, at the picnic, she'd come to a difficult conclusion. She couldn't live with herself if she let another man die. She felt responsible for Jaime, and her father, and the stranger in Puerto Escondido.

If something happened to Brandon, she'd be devastated.

When they arrived at the bottom of the valley, Carranza's men were nowhere to be seen. Darkness had fallen but the graveyard was bright with burning candles. Their soft glow warmed the starless night.

Brandon grasped her hand, his face lit up with hope. He thought they were going to make it. Isabel's heart tightened with sorrow and the flames blurred before her eyes. Together, they hurried toward the procession.

"Wait," she said, tugging his arm. "I need to rest."

He removed a bottle of water from his backpack and offered it to her.

She drank quickly, swallowing past the lump in her throat. "There's something I have to tell you before we go on."

He took a measured sip. "What?"

"You've been the best time of my life. Thank you."

Heat flickered in his blue eyes, along with an emotion she couldn't identify. "I haven't even started to show you a good time, angel."

She smiled through her tears. Touching his shadowed jaw, she gave him a lingering kiss. It tasted like lonely nights and lost wishes, and a thirst that could never be slaked. "I'm sorry," she whispered, licking her lips.

"For what?"

"This." Drawing back her fist, she sank it into his unsuspecting belly, sucker punching him as hard as she could.

He grunted in pain, holding one hand to his abs. His other hand locked around her wrist, lightning-quick. But this time she'd anticipated the move. Twisting out of his grip, she spun away from him and took off running.

Knowing she only had a few seconds' head start, she darted around a tall grave site. Grabbing a pale blue shawl from the headstone, she put it on her head like a veil. Heart racing, she plucked a burning candle from the ground and joined the procession.

Shoulder to shoulder with a similarly garbed woman, she shuffled forward, humming religious hymns.

Chapter 12

The dead walked among the living.

Isabel hunched her back and kept her chin down, trying to appear humble and wizened. From behind lowered lashes, she scanned the crowd for Carranza's men. She knew they were looking for her. Without Brandon, whose height set him apart, she'd be harder to spot, but that wasn't why she'd left him.

Splitting up was for his own good.

The drug cartel members were determined and resourceful. They wouldn't quit. She no longer believed she'd be safe in Guatemala. She was a hazard to everyone around her, and she refused to put Brandon's life at risk for another moment.

The women beside Isabel murmured prayers in Spanish, undisturbed by her presence. She'd never been to a celebration like this and wasn't sure what to expect. It was like a funeral procession, a holiday parade and a street carnival rolled into one. Hundreds of revelers carried brilliant bouquets of marigolds, brightly lit candles and colorful signs. Many were dressed in ragged clothes, their faces painted to resemble skulls. Dancing skeletons weaved through the throng, having a grand old time.

Isabel's head swam with merry music and raucous images of the afterlife. For this culture, death was a joyous occasion. The journey to the underworld was accompanied by singing mariachis and stomping feet.

Living was a trial; dying, the reward.

Although she couldn't share the sentiment right now, while she was fighting to survive, she did feel a certain sense of closure. Lighting a candle for her father had been therapeutic. Telling Brandon her story, even more so.

She hoped he wouldn't hate her for this. The thought of never seeing him again made tears rush into her eyes, so she pushed it aside and focused on moving forward. She put one foot in front of the other, whispering fervent prayers in Spanish.

She hadn't gone far when she caught a glimpse of the man with the broken nose. He was standing on a raised platform near the center square, wearing a black cowboy hat. Pulse racing, she put her head down and prayed harder. There was no way to make a break for it without attracting attention. A moment later, Brandon passed her on the opposite side, walking at a swifter pace than the rest of the crowd.

He was heading straight for the platform.

Her mind shouted a warning, but she couldn't call out or approach him without giving them both away. While she watched in horror, he strode down the street, frantically searching for her, heedless of his own safety. If he noticed Carranza's man, he didn't show it. He was acting like such a fool!

She'd counted on him being calm, cool and collected as always. He was ruining everything, taking a shocking risk.

Then it occurred to her that he would never do this without weighing the consequences. He wasn't really looking for her. He was trying to draw Carranza's thugs out. While they were busy chasing him, she could get away.

He hurried by the man in the black hat, not even glancing up at him. His feigned ignorance was so obvious Isabel wanted to scream. Brandon was trying to thwart her plans to save him by sacrificing himself. The sneaky bastard!

Carranza's man joined the procession and started following him immediately.

Incensed, she tossed aside her veil and picked up speed, startling the women next to her. When she was within striking distance, she drew back her arm and let the fat wax candle fly through the air, pegging the man in the black hat. He whirled to face her, his eyes wide. She turned and ran, her heart in her throat.

The smiling skulls and happy skeletons seemed more threatening now. Every colorful bouquet was an obstacle, every classical guitar a hooking weapon. She overturned signs and spilled baskets, jostling tipsy men and pious women. The man in the black hat raced after her, his heavy footsteps pounding. But she was smaller and more nimble, lengthening the distance between them with every stride.

When the opportunity presented itself, she made a sharp detour around the corner of a building, trying to shake him. She continued to run, her chest burning and her feet aching. Finally, she stopped on a deserted side street, struggling for breath. There was a black SUV parked nearby, its front windshield missing.

Oh, no.

Stomach sinking, she backed up slowly, preparing to retrace her steps. And gasped as she felt the cold bite of metal against her neck.

"Don't move," the voice behind her said. It was the other man, the one she'd hit over the head in the hotel carport parking garage. Keeping the barrel of the weapon pressed to her nape, he patted her down with his other hand, locating her dagger. "What's this?"

"Put away the gun and I'll show you."

He chuckled without humor, shoving her against the side of the building. "Little girls shouldn't play with big knives," he said, his English lightly accented. Sliding his hand into her pants, he removed the dagger from its sheath, letting the blade catch a glint of moonlight. "They can get cut."

Isabel didn't say anything. The man in the black hat would appear any minute, with Brandon hot on his trail.

"Come on," he said, dragging her toward the vehicle by the braids. She winced at the pain in her scalp but didn't cry out. When they reached the passenger door, he slammed her head into it. Black spots flashed before her eyes and the impact reverberated down her spine, weakening her knees.

She put up an ineffectual fight as he holstered his weapon, securing her wrists behind her back with coarse rope. When he pushed her into the passenger seat, she rallied, kicking him in the face as hard as she could.

"Bitch," he sputtered, stumbling backward.

Although the move didn't give her a chance to escape, her chest swelled with pride, because she'd busted his lip. Clearly he was displeased with her for hitting him over the head with a brick. He should have been prepared for her fractiousness.

The man with the broken nose came running toward the SUV, his hat gone. Brandon wasn't following him.

"Where's the *güero?*" his partner asked, spitting on the sidewalk.

"I took care of him."

"Good. Let's go."

While the bigger man climbed inside the vehicle, Isabel was thrown into the backseat, her heart cold with dread. Was Brandon hurt, or dying? Her world spun on its axis and shuddered to a grinding halt.

Please, no. Not Brandon. Anyone but him.

She stared out the window as they pulled away, traveling through an indecipherable maze of side streets because the main road was closed. Although she wanted Brandon to save himself, not her, she kept her eyes peeled, hoping to see him.

He didn't come.

Numbness settled over her, allowing her to endure the pain. She resolved to be as combative as possible. Carranza's men were taking her somewhere to kill her, and she wasn't going willingly. Scooting across the backseat, she fumbled for the door handle, her fingers straining. The rope at her wrists held tight, burning her skin. They hit a bump in the road and she almost went sprawling.

Gritting her teeth, she inched toward the door handle and tried again, her fingertips slipping over it without success. The driver pressed a button on the control panel, locking her in with an ominous click.

Isabel decided the driver needed another swift kick to the head. If she caused an accident, she might have a better chance of escaping.

"Tie up her feet," he said, glancing in the rearview mirror.

His partner grabbed the length of rope, giving her a

warning look as he reached for her ankles. Instead of struggling, she tried to appear soft and helpless, hoping the bigger man would be more sympathetic to a female in distress. He was the muscle in this operation, not the brains. Maybe he didn't enjoy hurting women.

The big man tied her feet securely and ignored her pleading gaze, telling her everything she needed to know. He wouldn't help her.

For the remainder of the ride, she searched for a cutting tool, her fingers digging into every nook and cranny of the backseat. There were pieces of safety glass from the shattered windshield on the floor, just out of reach. It was maddening.

"Where are we going?" she asked, noticing a sign that said *Zona Archeológica*.

Neither man replied.

The driver continued toward the grounds of some ancient ruins. Apparently, the remote location suited his needs. It was a perfect place to hide a body. There was no one around for miles, no one to hear her scream.

A chill shuddered down her spine.

The driver barreled through the front gate, breaking the chain lock. He continued past a group of stone pyramids and an abandoned ball court, parking beside a structure Isabel recognized as an underground tomb.

Fighting was futile, but she bucked wildly as they dragged her out of the vehicle. Her shrill cry was swallowed by the sultry night. She'd be tortured and buried here, among the souls of ancient warriors.

The big man shoved her down the steps of the tomb, ignoring the *Prohibido* sign at the entrance. She was forced into an underground room with a low ceiling and a dirt floor. There were several engraved stone tablets leaning against the wall, but no human remains.

Not yet.

The smaller man struck her across the face, knocking her down. With no arms to break her fall, she took a hard tumble. Pain spread from her cheek and the taste of blood filled her mouth. She curled up on her side, protecting her vital organs.

"That was for kicking me," the man said, as if his action had settled the score.

Isabel begged to differ. By her calculations, she still owed him one.

The large man stood by the entrance, keeping watch while his partner crouched beside her, flipping open his cell phone.

"What do you want?" she asked.

"Maybe we want to stuff pills down your throat until you choke," he answered, giving her a hard smile. His fingertips made a trail across her dusty cheek, tracing her lips. "I think I'd enjoy filling your pretty mouth."

"Try it," she invited, baring her teeth.

"We have her," he said into the phone, then listened for a response. *"Bueno."* Pressing a button, he turned the screen toward Isabel, letting her look. A man who resembled Jaime was there, staring back at her. It was his father, Manuel Carranza.

"I need to know what happened to my son," he said.

Isabel had never been on a video conference call. She struggled to an upright position, sitting in the dirt.

"If you tell me the truth, I'll let you go. You have my word."

"Your word means nothing to me," she said, incredulous.

"Please," he added, his eyes so much like Jaime's that she felt haunted by them. "I want to hear about his last moments. I have to understand why he died."

She fell silent, weighing her options. There was no benefit in cooperating. They'd kill her no matter what she said.

"Maybe I'll pay a visit to your mother," Carranza said. "From what I've heard, she's quite desperate to find you. I think she'd agree to meet with me."

Her stomach tightened with fear. "Leave her alone."

"Talk to me and I will."

She'd rather die resisting, standing strong. But she couldn't take the chance that he'd go after her mother. Brandon might be bleeding in an alleyway, or lying dead, because of her. Agony spread through her chest, threatening to suffocate her. She'd already hurt so many people she loved. Her mother was the only family member she had left.

"Do you promise?" she asked, although she didn't trust him.

"Of course. I don't enjoy harming women."

Taking a ragged breath, she agreed to talk. After a long moment, she lifted her chin, preparing to unsettle him with the disturbing story. She hoped he would choke on it. "I met Jaime at Club Deuce in Hollywood. He went there to socialize and sell drugs. I was one of his best customers."

Carranza waited for her to continue, his brow furrowed.

"On the night he…died, he seemed upset, as if a problem was bothering him. I bought him a few drinks, trying to cheer him up. He said he appreciated my company because I didn't hang all over him like the other girls."

A hint of resistance flickered in Carranza's eyes. Perhaps, deep down, he already knew where this was going.

"Jaime wanted to leave so we took a cab to my place. I'm not clear about what happened after that, but I remember one important detail."

"What?"

"He had a new wristband," she said, shifting her own wrists behind her back. "Like a brass cuff. He said you ordered him to take it off because it wasn't masculine. He tried to come out to you, but you wouldn't listen—"

"No," Carranza interrupted. "You're mistaken."

"You wouldn't listen," she repeated, more firmly this time. "But I did. I hugged him when he told me and I said it was okay. He didn't show much emotion and we were both so high...I thought he was fine."

His expression was guarded, his eyes full of pain. "Did you give him the pills?"

"I don't know," she said. She couldn't recall anything beyond the heartfelt conversation. "I think he found them after I feel asleep. I'm sure he was familiar with the drug and understood the dosage. He wouldn't have taken so many on accident."

"You're lying," Carranza roared.

"I'm sorry," she said, tears spilling down her cheeks. "I wish I could have helped him."

He looked away, cursing under his breath. He knew she was telling the truth. She saw it in his face. But he couldn't accept Jaime for who he was. He refused to acknowledge that his son had killed himself because he was gay.

"What do you want us to do?" the smaller man asked Carranza.

"Get rid of her," he said, and hung up.

Isabel stared at her captors, horrified. She had known it would end this way but couldn't hold back a sob of dismay. Dying here was her worst nightmare. She'd be trapped, alone in this dark tomb, for eternity.

Both of Carranza's men were aware of her innocence. They understood that the drug lord considered her a thorn in his side, not a threat to his organization. "Please," she said, reduced to begging. "You know this is wrong."

The big man appeared unenthusiastic about the task he was about to perform, but resigned to it. His comrade had a more sadistic bent. He studied her with cold anticipation, enamored with the idea of breaking her.

"He'll kill you, too," she said, panicking. "Now that you've heard Jaime's secret, he'll kill you, too!"

The smaller man took Isabel's dagger from his belt, testing its sharpness with his fingertip. "Stand guard outside."

His partner hesitated, glancing at her prone form.

"Do you want to watch me do it?"

"A bullet would be cleaner."

"And easier to trace."

The big man shifted, uncomfortable with the situation. Even cold-blooded murderers were reluctant to kill defenseless young women. He didn't like this job, and he didn't appear to like his partner.

"You're next," Isabel promised. "He'll lay you out beside me."

"Go on," the smaller man said, dismissing him. "I'll make it quick."

After a brief pause, her last hope turned his back on her. He ascended the stone steps, disappearing into the night.

Chapter 13

Brandon was too late.

It took him several seconds to recover after Isabel socked him in the gut. He hadn't expected the move and she'd executed it perfectly. As soon as he caught his breath, he took off running, scanning the crowded cemetery for her. It was almost as if she'd vanished into thin air. He cut through the procession, searching for her fleeing form. Although he stood taller than most of the men and all of the women, he couldn't see her.

She'd given him the slip.

When it dawned on him that she was hiding amidst the townspeople, he started looking for a woman of her size and stature, with no luck. Half of the girls in the town had dark, braided hair and slender figures. He would have had to study hundreds of faces to find her, and many of the young ladies kept their eyes downcast. Giving every

female a close examination would attract too much attention from protective husbands and fathers.

Growing frantic, and increasingly disturbed by the
cheery images of death, he moved to the side of the street.
Some of the men were watching the festivities, drinking
cold cerveza. Gaucho Rodriguez was standing with them,
ill-concealed in a tall cowboy hat. Brandon walked past
him and ducked behind a building, his heart racing. When
Gaucho didn't take the bait, Brandon doubled back, curious. He'd gone the opposite direction.

Damn it.

Brandon sprinted hard but didn't catch anything but a
black cowboy hat, still warm, discarded in haste. As he
rounded the corner, he saw the SUV weaving through side
streets, brake lights flashing. Isabel was in the backseat.
He picked up the pace, trying to close the distance, but he
couldn't run as fast as a moving vehicle.

It turned onto a lonely road, leaving him in the dust.

He threw down the cowboy hat and sank to his knees,
howling with frustration. In the blink of an eye, he'd lost
her. He'd let the target fall into enemy hands. And like a
damned fool, he'd fallen in love with her.

He'd fallen in *love* with her.

Cursing violently, he scrambled to his feet. He couldn't
let a couple of ruthless criminals steal his woman. But he
didn't have many options. Calling the local police would
be suicidal and no other assistance was available.

He glanced around for a car to steal, raking a hand
through his hair. A man on a bicycle pedaled down a deserted cross street, oblivious to his plight. "Hey," Brandon
shouted, waving the hat in the air. "Help!"

The man slowed, but didn't stop.

"I have money," Brandon said, jogging toward him.

"Mucho dinero!" Proving it, he took a wad of bills out of his pocket.

The man on the bike pedaled forward, curious. He had a metal basket filled with pink candy skulls. Brandon couldn't imagine a less appetizing treat. He pictured children munching on blood-colored icing and jelly-filled brains.

"Give me your bike," he said, thrusting the cash at him. "You can have the hat, the money, the shirt off my back."

The man accepted the deal, nodding his agreement. The bike wasn't new but the hat was. Along with the dollar bills, it was a fair trade. Brandon waited, his heart leaping with hope, while the man climbed off the bike and removed his belongings from the basket. His weathered hands were clumsy, and he smelled like tequila.

Brandon's patience broke. He wrenched the wire basket off the bike and set it aside. Several sugar skulls tumbled out, rolling down the street. "Sorry, I'm in a hurry," he said, pointing after the SUV. "Where does that road go?"

The man blinked at it, bleary. "Izapa."

"Izapa?"

He formed a triangle with his hands, making the shape of a pyramid. *"Las ruínas."*

The ruins.

"Thank you," Brandon said, and took off, pedaling hard. The bike was old but sturdy, and it had good tires. It was faster than his legs, and there was no other transportation around. He could only hope for steep downhill grades.

They didn't come easy. For what seemed like an hour, he toiled uphill, sweating like crazy and cursing the entire country of Mexico. The humidity was killing him. What kind of godforsaken place celebrated death? Every man, woman and child in Tapachula must have been walking in the parade, because the outskirts of town were eerily quiet. There wasn't a car on the road, not a single wandering soul.

At long last, the most evil hill in the universe descended into a cool, dark valley. Without the glimmer of moonlight, he'd never have been able to pick up speed. The danger of hitting a rock and flying over the cliff was still considerable, but he accepted the risk with relish, baring his teeth to the night.

Finally, he was making good time.

Carranza's men wanted to question Isabel. He knew that, and prayed she would drag the process out by failing to cooperate. She was good at staying mum, even better at kicking ass. God, he loved her. And, if they lived through this, he was going to paddle her lovely backside for punching him.

Looking forward to it, he approached the ruins of Izapa. Blunt-topped pyramids rose up from a dark carpet of vegetation, gleaming like old bones in the moonlight. The ancient stone buildings loomed before him, stoic and impenetrable. A patina of moss specked the surfaces of the boulders, giving them a mottled appearance.

Brandon left his bike by the broken front gate and proceeded on foot, his weapon ready, heart thundering in his chest.

He passed a dozen structures before spotting the SUV. It was parked next to an underground dwelling or bunker of some sort. Ducking behind a mossy block wall, he studied the scene from a distance, deliberating the best method of attack. Gaucho was standing guard at the entrance of the bunker. Brandon could pick him off from here.

Sharpshooting wasn't part of his typical repertoire, but he wouldn't hesitate to take this scumbag out. His new mission was to save Isabel and nothing else mattered. He'd reassigned himself. The only problem was that a gunshot would alert the man inside the bunker and put Isabel at risk.

Deciding to employ stealth instead of shock, he dropped to his belly and army-crawled toward the SUV at an angle. Gaucho didn't see him. When he arrived at the vehicle, he stopped to listen. He couldn't hear anything but the buzz of insects and the faint ticking of the cooling system.

Rising carefully to a crouching position, he peered through the SUV's tinted side windows, which were still intact. Gaucho hadn't moved an inch.

Taking a small penknife out of his pocket, he stabbed it into the front tire, letting the air out with an audible hiss.

Gaucho turned his head toward the sound.

Brandon jerked the knife out of the tire and put it away quickly, holding his gun at the ready. When his opponent came around the front of the vehicle to check out the noise, Brandon advanced, cracking him across the temple with the butt of his weapon. Gaucho stumbled sideways but didn't go down.

Brandon gulped, retreating a step.

He'd delivered a solid, skull-rattling hit and the behemoth hadn't even fallen. But perhaps he was dazed, because he didn't call out or retaliate, just blinked at Brandon in befuddled fury.

Brandon hit him again, harder. Blood spurted from a tear in his scalp, streaking his stunned face. Making a gurgling sound, he sank to his knees in the grass and then careened forward, unconscious.

From somewhere underground, Isabel let out an ear-splitting shriek. Brandon switched off the safety and leaped into action.

* * *

Isabel rotated her wrists behind her back, exploring the rope's resistance as her captor came forward.

The coarse fibers bit into her skin and there was no room to maneuver. She couldn't feel the tips of her fingers. Her feet weren't bound as tightly. She flexed her ankles, praying for the knot to slip.

He gave her a slow perusal, proving he wasn't going to kill her quickly. "I've seen your picture in a magazine. Very nice."

She tried to work up enough saliva to spit in his eye, but her mouth was too dry. Watching him approach, she continued to saw her wrists and ankles, searching for a weak spot in the binding.

He shoved her down in the dirt, pressing his forearm to her throat. Her wrists were pinned underneath her body, crushed by their combined weight. Tears sprang into her eyes but she refused to give him the satisfaction of crying out.

Flashing a dark smile, he trailed the tip of her knife down the center of her chest, slicing the beautiful tunic in half. While he stared at her exposed breasts, she gritted her teeth and scissored her ankles. The rope loosened, little by little.

He lifted the blade to her cheek, tracing her trembling lips. "Shh," he said, as if this would calm her. "It will all be over soon."

She turned her head to the side, shuddering with revulsion. In her direct line of sight there was a stone engraving of an eagle, its talons clutching a bloody heart. She concentrated on the unsettling image, trying to draw strength from it.

Taking her silence as a sign of defeat, the man moved the knife to her drawstring waistband, cutting it away.

Channeling her fear and fury, she focused on the eagle's sharp talons and visualized the rope unraveling. Her attacker set aside the knife, fumbling with his trousers. The rope slipped down, freeing one foot.

Yes!

She brought her knee up, slamming it into his groin with all her might. He made a strangled sound and rolled off her, holding his injured parts. She kicked out wildly, bucking her body as the rope unraveled. Knowing she only had seconds to escape, she scooted away from him and struggled to her feet.

He grabbed her ankle, sending her sprawling.

This time she couldn't hold back her scream. She tried to tuck into the fall and was only partly successful. Her hip and shoulder bounced off the hard-packed earth, jarring her bones. The impact stunned her.

He leaped on her back and grabbed her by the hair, wrenching her head up and holding his gun to her temple. "I was going to leave your face intact, *puta*. Now even your mother won't recognize you."

Brandon appeared in the entranceway, his gun aimed at the man on top of her. Isabel's heart seized. "Drop it or die."

Instead of dropping it, her captor took the barrel away from Isabel's head and pointed it at Brandon. Shots discharged from both weapons and the tomb exploded in chaos. Ancient stone fragments flew in every direction, filling the space with dust. Her attacker loosened his grip on her hair and collapsed, trapping her beneath him. Warm wetness trickled down her neck. Brandon rushed forward, pushing the limp body off her.

Everything went silent. She felt like she was sobbing, but she couldn't hear a sound. The smell of gunshot residue filled her nostrils. Horrified, she turned to look at the carnage. Her captor was stretched out on his side, mouth open. The back of his head was missing. Gore splattered the stone walls.

Oh, my God.

Sickened by the sight, she hunched over and retched, her empty stomach revolting. Nothing came up but saliva. Her ears were ringing, her head spinning.

Brandon knelt beside her, cutting her wrists free. Her hands tingled with a bright, dizzying pain. His mouth moved but she couldn't make out the words. He urged her to her feet, yanking her pants up her hips. They left the tomb together.

She didn't want to get inside the SUV, but he insisted. While he drove away from the ruins, going as fast as he could with a flat tire, she started trembling uncontrollably. Tears rolled down her swollen cheek and the ache in her right ear reached a piercing crescendo.

Closing her eyes, she wished for drugs, for death, for oblivion.

Chapter 14

Brandon knew Isabel was in shock.

She hadn't said a word since they left the ruins, and she wasn't responding to his voice. He'd asked several times if she was hurt, to no avail. Her eyes were squeezed shut, her shoulders trembling, clothes in tatters.

Taking the quilt out of his backpack, he covered her half-exposed upper body.

Pelón Garcia had hit her. The angry red mark stood out on her cheek, plain as day. He'd also raped her, or attempted to rape her. Either way, Brandon was furious, his chest heaving with pent-up rage. If he could go back and kill the man again, he would. If he could make him suffer, draw it out and watch him bleed, he would.

Some of his anger was directed toward himself. He'd let her come to harm. She'd been hurt on his watch. That was unacceptable.

His mood black, he drove as close to the border as possible and pulled over, parking the vehicle near a tree-lined ravine. The front windshield was gone, safety glass scattered all over the interior. They couldn't slip into Guatemala unnoticed in a bullet-riddled SUV, and he wanted to distance himself from Carranza as much as possible. The vehicle probably had a GPS system. Brandon doubted that the man he'd knocked out would come after them tonight, but reinforcements might.

He took a bottle of water out of his backpack and offered it to Isabel. She didn't take it. When he touched her arm, she moaned, turning her head away.

Brandon wondered if she'd broken something. Her shirt was stained with the dead man's blood, her face pale from nausea. He got out of the driver's seat and walked around to the passenger side, opening the door. "Can you stand?"

She stared at his lips, miserable.

Frowning, he checked her upper body for injuries, starting at her fingertips. Her wrists were red from rope burns but he didn't find any obvious breaks. She slapped his hands aside and touched her right ear.

Understanding dawned. "Can you hear me?"

She shook her head.

Relief and sympathy washed over him. One of his buddies had ruptured an eardrum during a training exercise. The pain was debilitating, but temporary. He rummaged through his backpack, which held her first aid kit. There were some ibuprofen tablets inside. She took two with water, wincing as she swallowed.

"We have to go," he said, pointing at the road. She needed to see a doctor, but getting across the border was his top priority.

She nodded, sliding out of the passenger seat with his help. On her first step forward, she let out a little cry and swayed toward him, her knees buckling. He caught her as she fell, remembering that ear injuries caused dizziness. Securing the quilt around her body, he solved the problem by lifting her into his arms.

When she didn't argue, merely closed her eyes and put her head on his shoulder, he knew she was suffering.

He took off toward the border crossing, guided by moonlight. This late in the evening, there wasn't a single car on the road. He walked for about mile without slowing, and it was hard going, the most difficult trek of his life. She was slim but sleek with muscle, not delicate. His biceps burned from bearing her weight.

Finally a car happened by, its driver slowing to offer them a ride. Brandon pretended not to understand any Spanish and the man stopped asking questions. They crossed the bridge into Guatemala without incident.

Isabel curled up against him and slept.

"Hay hospital en San Marcos," the driver said, glancing in his rearview mirror.

Brandon made a vague noise of agreement, brushing a lock of hair from Isabel's brow. His heart swelled with a mixture of emotions. He was so grateful she was alive, but deeply disturbed by the trauma she'd endured. By the skin of his teeth, he'd gotten them out of Mexico. Now that the mission was almost complete, he felt sick about the final step. He couldn't bear to betray her while she was vulnerable.

The trip to San Marcos, the largest city in the region, took several hours. As they neared the business center, Isabel roused, looking out the window. The rest had done her good. When he offered her water, she drank eagerly.

"Feel better?"

"Much. I can hear again."

"With both ears?"

She frowned, touching her right side. "This one still hurts a little. And you sound quiet, far away."

He didn't know if her hearing loss would be permanent, but he was glad she was responding to his voice again.

The driver cruised by a small medical facility, which was closed. He continued on to a budget hotel, saying the owner would give them a fair price. Brandon offered him some cash, but he wouldn't take it.

"Vaya con Dios," he said, nodding at Isabel.

She murmured the proper response, mustering a weak smile. Brandon helped her out of the backseat and she walked to the front entrance of the hotel without assistance. While she stood in the lobby, quilt around her shoulders, he paid for a room.

He knew he should go straight to the authorities, documents in hand. He'd killed one man and seriously injured another. Even in his line of work, which was fraught with risk, fatalities were unusual. His boss would need full, immediate disclosure.

But the only thing he cared about was Isabel.

Too exhausted to weigh the consequences, he climbed into bed with her as soon as they entered the room. Holding her close, he listened to her soft, steady breathing, his chest aching with tenderness.

Moments later, he was asleep.

When Isabel opened her eyes, Brandon wasn't there.

She turned to look for him, moving her head gingerly. The room was bright with daylight, and empty except for her. The pain in her ear had receded into a vague discomfort but every muscle in her body ached. She felt like she'd surfed the pipeline all day and been mashed against the reef. Repeatedly.

Violent images from the night before assaulted her,

flashing through her mind like a horror film reel. She felt dirty, hollow, deeply disturbed. Blood and gore had dried on her shirt, stiffening the fabric.

Cringing, she rose from the bed.

Brandon's backpack was still there, so she figured he'd gone out to get breakfast. Her stomach rumbled with hunger, indifferent to trauma. She stretched her arms over her head, trying to ease her sore muscles.

What she needed was a warm bath. Grabbing her messenger bag, she padded into the bathroom, which boasted a nice-size tub. Letting the water run hot, she discarded her ruined clothes and examined her appearance. The scrape on her cheek wasn't that bad. She brushed her teeth, glad they were intact.

Unbraiding her hair, she slipped into the tub, rested her head on the edge and soaked the terrifying experience away.

When she was clean, she felt like a new woman. In some ways, last night had been cathartic. She'd been forced to come to terms with Jaime's death. Speaking openly about his final moments had prompted an epiphany: she wasn't responsible for every tragedy that had befallen her. She *was* responsible for the way she'd reacted. There was nothing healthy about wallowing in guilt or avoiding consequences.

It was time to face the music.

She combed her hair until it gleamed and wrapped a towel around her well-scrubbed, slightly battered body before walking out into the main room. Brandon was sitting at the table, sipping coffee. The *pan de muerto* he'd bought at the fair rested on the surface, along with a couple of shopping bags.

Although she was hungry, her gaze stayed on him. He looked rumpled and road-weary and good enough to eat.

"You showered," he said, skimming her bare legs.

She sat down across from him, tearing off a hunk of bread. It was sweet, like a doughnut, and dusted with sugar. The grains dissolved on her tongue. "Mmm-hmm."

"Where are your clothes?"

"In the trash."

He studied her bruised cheek. "How do you feel?"

"Not too bad, considering." She tasted the coffee, appreciating its bold flavor. "How about you? Did you sleep?"

"I got a few hours," he said, rolling the tension from his shoulders.

The noise she made in response sounded like wifely disapproval. She flushed a little, warmed by the notion.

"Do you want to see a doctor?"

"No."

"You need medical attention."

"I'm fine. The earache passed."

His eyes searched hers, delving deeper, for emotional scars. "You were assaulted," he said quietly.

"Do I look awful?"

"You look beautiful. Did he rape you?"

"No," she said, touching the mark on her face. "You stopped him."

"I killed him," he corrected.

She didn't flinch at the harsh words. "I'm glad."

He stared at her for a moment, a muscle in his jaw flexing. Something about this conversation bothered him and it wasn't the attempted rape. Although he'd saved her life, he seemed uncomfortable in the role of hero.

Or maybe he didn't think there was anything heroic about shooting a man and watching his head explode.

"Thank you," she said anyway, her throat tight.

He acknowledged her statement with a curt nod, taking another sip of coffee. "I have to shower."

She watched him leave the table, upset with herself. She was sorry she'd put him through such a horrifying ordeal, and regretted hurting him in the graveyard. But she couldn't take the blame for another unfortunate death. Carranza's men had attacked her—they'd brought this outcome on themselves.

He picked up one of the shopping bags and ducked into the bathroom. When the shower turned on, she blinked out of her stupor. Taking a deep breath, she finished her breakfast. Brandon knew it was dangerous to come after her, and she was damned lucky he had. She owed him an apology…and so much more.

He came out of the bathroom a few minutes later, smelling like steamy male skin and soap lather. The pants he was wearing were too short, barely reached his ankles. With no shirt or shoes, he looked like a sexy castaway.

She smiled behind her coffee cup, enjoying the view.

"I bought clothes for you, too," he said, pointing at the other bag.

"Really?" Touched by his thoughtfulness, she rose from the table, perusing the contents. A pair of simple black flip-flops. Plain white panties, a size too large. She forgave the mistake when she saw a green cotton sundress. Making a soft exclamation of pleasure, she brought the garment to her chest, whirling to face the mirror above the dresser.

"Ouch," she said, almost stumbling on her tender foot.

"What is it?"

"Blisters," she replied, admiring the soft fabric. "This is lovely."

He grabbed the first aid kit and sat at the edge of the bed, gesturing for her foot. She boosted herself up on the dresser, stretching her leg out to him. He dabbed ointment on every tiny sore, and smoothed more on the rope burns around her ankles. Then he applied a couple of bandage strips as needed.

"Thanks," she said when he was finished, wiggling her toes.

His gaze traveled up her bare legs, lingering at the hem of her towel. "You're welcome," he said gruffly, rising from the bed.

She reached out to stop him. There were so many thoughts and emotions spinning around her head. It was difficult to sort them all out. "I'm sorry I hit you yesterday. Believe it or not, I was trying to protect you."

He remained silent, neither accepting nor rejecting her apology.

She toyed with his hand, self-conscious. "I've decided to travel to the embassy and turn myself in."

"When?"

"Tomorrow, I guess."

"Why wait?"

She looked up at him, her pulse pounding. "Because I can't stand the thought of leaving this room without touching you."

His eyes darkened with understanding.

"I have to take control of my life," she said, raising her hand to his jaw. His whiskers there were rough-soft against her fingertips. "But first, I want to be yours. I need to feel alive, just once, before I go."

He swallowed hard, studying her face. Judging by his pained expression, he wasn't unaffected by her confession.

She dropped her hands to the knot between her breasts, letting the towel fall away. His gaze trailed downward, moving from her exposed breasts to the dark triangle between her thighs in an agonizingly slow drag. Her nipples tightened at the visual caress. She tilted her head back, parting her lips in invitation.

"You were attacked last night," he said, putting his mouth close to hers.

"Yes."

"This isn't a good way to deal with trauma."

"Maybe it's the best way."

Still, he hesitated. "I don't think I can be gentle."

She couldn't wait.

When she nodded her acceptance, he thrust his hand into her hair, taking her mouth in a plundering kiss. There was no tenderness, as promised. Only heat, and need, and domination. She reveled in his taste, gripping the underside of the dresser. Their tongues met and tangled, mouths wide open.

Then he broke the kiss, panting. "Hold that thought." Giving her a hungry look, he strode across the room, shrugging into his shirt.

"Where are you going?"

"Condoms. There's a drugstore around the corner." Leaving his shirt unbuttoned and his boot laces untied, he flew out the door. She waited for him to return, her heart racing with excitement. Should she stay like this, buck naked on the dresser? Feeling anxious, she turned to the side, examining her reflection in the mirror. Her popularity as a bikini model had been more about her father's notoriety than her specific measurements. She'd never had lush hips or big breasts. But she was proud of her athletic body and didn't regret the sexy photo shoots.

Brandon had said she was beautiful. Those words had always seemed empty to her. Now she felt warmed by them, from the inside out.

Closing her eyes, she vowed to enjoy their final moments together. This was her last day of freedom, her last chance to experience pleasure. She was going to make the most of it, to grab happiness with both hands.

When Brandon burst through the door, her breath caught in her throat. Eyes cruising over her nude form, he tossed a box of condoms on the bed, wrestled out of his shirt and kicked off his boots.

Her tummy quivered in anticipation.

He stepped up to the dresser, ready to pick up where they left off. Moving a lock of hair off her shoulder, he pressed his lips to her bare skin.

"I've never done it this way before," she said, shivering.

He went still. "What way?"

She laughed, resting her forehead against his chest. "Sober. I've never done it sober. The details are kind of fuzzy."

"No problem," he said, smiling a little. "I'll give you a refresher course."

"How nice of you."

"I'm in a generous mood."

She giggled helplessly as he lifted her off the dresser, falling across the bed with her. Then he covered her mouth with his, kissing the last of her inhibitions away. "I think I remember a few things," she said, sprawling over him.

"Do you?"

Nodding, she explored the bunched muscles in his shoulders. "I like this," she said, touching the hair on his chest.

"Hmm."

Moving on, she traced the trail down his stomach, kissing his flat abdomen. "I'm sorry I hurt you."

He groaned, threading his hand through her hair.

His erection was clearly outlined beneath the fabric of his trousers, standing at full attention. She moistened her lips, studying the broad tip and rigid length. Licking his hard belly, she molded her palm around him.

He inhaled a sharp breath, his abdominals tight as a drum.

"Maybe I can make it up to you," she said in a husky voice. Lowering his zipper, she freed him from the restrictive barrier. Curling her hand around his shaft, she stroked him up and down. Her insides went molten as she took him into her mouth. He watched her intently, his grip on her hair tightening. She moaned, swirling her tongue around him.

"Wait," he said, pulling her head away from his groin. "That feels amazing, but I can't handle it right now."

She'd been thrilled by the sensation of having him in her mouth and wanted to continue. But when he stretched out on top of her and pinned her arms over her head, kissing her senseless, she forgot her disappointment.

"You can do that later," he promised.

"I want to do everything," she said, panting against his lips. "I want you everywhere."

That statement gave him pause. "Everywhere in the room, or everywhere on your body?"

"Both," she decided.

With a hoarse chuckle, he glanced around, imagining the possibilities. "In that case, get back up on the dresser."

A thrill raced through her. She slid off the bed, doing his bidding.

Cheeks flushed with passion, he followed her, bringing the condoms with him. His erection was jutting at his open fly, inviting her to touch. Instead of suiting up, he set the box down and stepped between her parted legs, kissing her mouth again and again. He cupped her breasts, trapping her stiff nipples between his thumb and forefinger. With every firm pinch, her sex tightened in response, aching to be filled.

She reached into his pants, wrapping her fingers around his thick erection. "I want this. Please."

"I'm going to give it to you, honey. Believe me."

"Hurry."

Eyes glittering, he pushed her hands aside and sank to his knees before her. She felt embarrassingly slick and swollen, her nipples pebble-hard. Holding her gaze, he kissed her trembling inner thigh. She moaned, spreading her legs wider.

When he dipped his head to taste her, she gasped in delight, clutching at his short hair. She'd never been so aroused in her life. Licking his lips slowly, he slid a blunt finger inside her. "You're so pretty here."

She squirmed on the dresser, begging for more.

His mouth settled on her and all rational thought fled. He flicked his tongue over her tender flesh, worrying the taut nub and stroking her with his fingers until she screamed, shattering into a thousand pieces. His touch gentled as the last of the tremors faded. She felt like a puddle of sensitive nerve endings, boneless.

He stood, removing his glistening fingers from her before putting on the condom. "You still want this?"

She nodded, twining her arms around his neck. Her orgasm had been explosive but she needed more to feel complete. He guided himself into her inch by inch. She struggled to accommodate him, gasping at the over-whelming sense of fullness.

When he was buried to the hilt, he let out a strangled groan. "You feel so good. I can't last."

She wrapped her legs around him, desperate for him to move.

After giving her a moment to adjust, he eased himself back and forth, her moisture making him slick. She looked down at their joined bodies, mesmerized by the erotic sight. "Isabel," he choked, sliding in and out.

Her pouty nipples rubbed against his rough chest hair and his pelvis bumped hers with every thrust. It was almost too much pleasure to bear. She dug her fingernails into his shoulders and threw her head back, sobbing his name. He glanced at her face, as if gauging her proximity to climax. Licking his thumb, he placed it over her sensitive nub, helping her along.

With a keening cry, she came again, her sex pulsing around him.

He swiveled her from the dresser to the bed in one fluid motion and fell on top of her, thrusting hard. She studied his clenched jaw and flexing muscles, excited beyond belief. He felt huge and hot inside her, reaching depths no one else had.

She'd never been so fiercely loved.

Gritting his teeth, he pounded into her until he found his own release, his body shuddering against hers. When it was over, he disposed of the condom and came back to bed, drawing her into his arms. She closed her eyes and rested her head on his chest, listening to the sound of his beating heart.

Chapter 15

Isabel rose from the bed at sundown.

Brandon was stretched out on his stomach, fast asleep. The sheet rode low on his hips, revealing most of his naked body. His shoulders bore crescent marks from her fingernails, made in the throes of passion. She watched him for a moment, wondering if he was dreaming of her. They'd spent most of the day making love. After exhausting their condom supply, and themselves, they collapsed in a tangle of sweaty limbs and twisted sheets. She'd never felt so satisfied. He'd finally relaxed enough to drift off with her.

He was sprawled across the bed, all long legs and lean muscles, his face boyish in repose. She studied the edge of his shadowed jaw, aching to kiss him one last time. To curl up beside him and forget the world outside.

When her vision blurred, she tore her gaze away from him, taking a slow breath. The dress he'd bought her was hanging over a chair. She put on the underwear and flip-flops, both of which fitted loose, and pulled the dress over her head. It was a simple style, sort of Grecian, with a high waist and a V-necked bodice. Hands trembling, she tamed her wild hair into a sleek knot at her nape and picked up her messenger bag, ready to go.

It was better to leave now and make a clean break. For his protection, she wouldn't mention his name to the authorities.

On her way out the door, she hesitated. She hadn't planned to write a note but it seemed cold not to. Their time together had been incredibly special. After everything they'd been through, she owed him a goodbye.

She found notebook paper in her bag. Moving quietly, she rifled through his backpack, checking the zippered pockets for a pen or pencil. Her fingertips brushed over a piece of fabric that felt familiar. She removed it, recognizing the strip of linen she'd used as a washcloth. Although logic told her he'd needed a handkerchief, not something to remember her by, her stomach fluttered at the sight. This scrap of fabric symbolized the sensuality he'd awoken in her. It evoked deep longing and uncontrollable desire.

Setting the linen aside, she reached farther into the backpack, locating a strange little pocket at the bottom. Inside there was a flat metal disk. Frowning, she took the object out of the pack and read its shiny surface.

>Deputy Marshal Brandon Knox
>International Fugitive Task Force Division
>United States Marshals Service

Smothering her cry of outrage, she turned to stare at the stranger on the bed. He'd tricked her. Everything he'd said was a lie. He was a *cop,* not a tourist.

How could she have been such a fool?

For several long, drawn-out seconds, she considered grabbing the gun out of his bag and pointing it at him, demanding answers. Maybe he had a pair of handcuffs. It would serve him right if she locked him to the bed and left him here, naked and vulnerable.

The urge to make him pay was intense. She struggled with it, tears of shock and anger filling her eyes.

In the end, she resisted temptation. He'd slept very little for the past few days and might not wake for hours on his own. It was better to sneak away now, leaving him in the dark. Grimacing, she replaced the badge in his pack.

She crept across the room and slipped through the door, pausing outside to see if he would follow. When he didn't appear, she took off at a brisk pace, hurrying down the street. She asked the first person she saw for directions to the bus station. Luckily, it was less than a mile away. As soon as she arrived she bought an express ticket to Guatemala City. The last bus was scheduled to depart as she made the purchase. She ran to catch it.

The next few hours passed in a blur. Her chest ached with emptiness. Earlier today, in Brandon's arms, she'd felt so complete. His touch had affected her on so many levels. Their eyes had met, over and over again, while he was inside her. Every kiss was a revelation, every caress an unspoken promise to love her forever. She didn't think she'd imagined the emotional connection. He hadn't just showed her how he felt, he'd *told* her. Some of it was dirty talk and sweet nothings, but everything he'd said sounded sincere.

Was it all a lie?

She couldn't bear to evaluate every personal detail he'd shared with her. Maybe he'd invented his entire life story to meet her needs, adopting traits he knew she would find attractive. Her cheeks burned at the thought. She felt crushed, used, desperate. Like one of her father's groupies, man-hungry and easy to manipulate.

Blinking the tears from her eyes, she focused on her next step. She refused to be derailed by this...setback. She'd fled to Mexico to protect herself, physically and emotionally. That period of her life was over.

She'd been hurt again—so what? She was tired of playing the victim, ready to leave the past behind her.

It was after midnight when she arrived in Guatemala City. She had just enough money for bus fare to the embassy in the morning. Entering the transit center, she found a hard plastic chair to curl up in and closed her eyes.

Alone, once again.

Brandon woke up in the dark.

He lifted his head and looked around the shadowy hotel room, aware that Isabel was no longer beside him. The bathroom door stood open, revealing an empty interior.

She was gone.

Lurching to his feet, he kicked away the tangled sheets and turned on the lights, blinking at the sudden brightness. Her messenger bag was missing, along with the clothes he'd bought. His backpack was on the floor, unzipped. The washcloth he'd taken as a memento had been thrown out like an old rag.

Damn.

Heart hammering against his ribs, he checked the backpack's contents. His badge and documents were still hidden, but she might have seen them. A blank sheet of paper, torn from her small notebook, rested on the table. He crushed it in his fist, making a strangled sound of frustration.

"Stupid," he muttered under his breath, wanting to

punch a hole in the wall. Of all the mistakes he'd made in his life, this ranked number one. He'd been so close to completing his mission and escorting Isabel back to the U.S. safely. But he'd thrown it away for a couple of hot hours in bed.

He was a disgrace.

Furious with himself, he got dressed quickly, cursing his ill-fitting trousers and overactive libido. He stuffed their dirty clothes in an empty trash bag and shoved it in his backpack, protecting the evidence. Then he tossed the key on the bed and walked out, leaving the door open behind him.

On the way to the bus station, it occurred to him that she might have planned this. The lonely sheet of paper suggested that she'd intended to write a goodbye note but changed her mind. She'd obviously searched through his belongings, and taken pains not to wake him. He was a light sleeper, even when exhausted.

If she'd meant to ditch him all along, then the story she told about needing his touch was just an ego-stroke. She'd screwed him into a coma on purpose. Had she faked her responses, stoking him further with breathy little moans and hoarse cries? He flushed, remembering some of the sappy things he'd said to her in the heat of the moment. All true.

Raking a hand through his hair, he approached the terminal, scanning the departure times for her most likely escape route. She couldn't go back to Mexico, and sticking around here was ill-advised. She'd probably gone to Guatemala City. It boasted an international airport, passenger trains and big crowds to hide among.

He'd track her down again.

The last bus to the capital had left earlier in the evening. Brandon stepped toward the ticket window, using his workmanlike Spanish to inquire about Isabel. Sure enough, the man behind the counter remembered a beautiful señorita in a green dress. Her striking looks were a blessing and a curse, weren't they?

The transit center offered rental car services. He paid for a midsize sedan. Armed with a road map and a large cup of coffee, he was ready to drive all night.

It was just before dawn when the city came into view, all rolling hills and ramshackle dwellings. Houses of every size and shape, many made of discarded construction materials, filled the landscape. The bus station and airport were situated on the outer edge of town. Although Isabel's bus had arrived hours ago, he went there first. She might be waiting for another departure.

He parked in a pay lot and bought a zippered sweatshirt from an outdoor vendor. Slouching a little, he put the hood up and entered the transit center. There were rows of stationary chairs as far as the eye could see, interspersed with tiny snack shops and international fast-food joints.

Scanning the crowd, he caught a glimpse of green. Isabel was curled up in a chair in a back row, her head resting on her tucked hands. She'd tied her hair back but a few tendrils had escaped, giving her a mussed appearance.

He studied her from a distance, memorizing every detail. For a fleeing fugitive, she wasn't well hidden. Her shoulders were slumped and her mouth downturned. Though her eyes were closed, he knew she was awake. She had tears on her face.

Brandon swore silently, his anger dissipating. He had a warrant for her arrest but he hesitated to use it. Maybe her abandonment was another misguided attempt to protect him. He wanted to believe that their encounter had meant something to her.

Obviously, he was an idiot—but he was still in love with her.

He sank into one of the chairs near the exit, his thoughts in turmoil. For her own safety, he couldn't let her go free. He had to complete the mission. Although he'd love to pass this final task on to an armed guard, and leave her with mostly positive memories of Brandon North, he couldn't shirk his duty.

Now that he knew Isabel, he understood how much she valued her freedom and independence. She'd felt trapped in Mexico, alone and isolated. She might be pissed at him for deceiving her, but she'd *hate* him for detaining her.

He shouldn't have touched her.

If he'd been able to control himself, his betrayal wouldn't be as painful. He should have been strong enough to resist. But when she'd dropped her towel, the blood had rushed from his head to his groin, and stayed there until he'd exhausted them both.

Smothering a groan, he clenched his hands into fists. Instead of approaching her, he remained seated, putting off the inevitable, sick with regret.

Isabel took the bus to the embassy at first light.

She was hungry and tired, her muscles aching from both pleasant activities and unpleasant ones. All night long she'd been plagued by hot-flash memories of Brandon's touch and cold-sweat worries about her future. Although her anxiety level had skyrocketed, her resolve hadn't wavered. She had to take the first step toward the rest of her life.

As she rode with a crowd of travelers to the downtown area, she glanced around warily, wondering if she was being followed. She didn't see anyone suspicious and didn't much care. There was no reason for stealth today.

She supposed she could have stayed at the hotel with Brandon. U.S. Marshals caught fugitives and brought them home. But she wanted to surrender on her own terms. Face this fate head-on, unflinching. And she certainly didn't mind depriving him of success. The outcome would be the same but she'd meet it with dignity.

Straightening her shoulders, she exited the bus and walked toward the small building. The embassy offices were inauspicious, rather than grand. As soon as she came through the entrance she was greeted by a guard and directed through a metal detector. Clearing security, she approached the front desk.

A pretty, dark-haired receptionist greeted her. "May I help you?"

"Yes," Isabel said, clearing her throat. "I'm an American citizen and I need to speak to the ambassador."

The receptionist offered a bland smile. "Ambassador Richards isn't in today, miss. He doesn't take walk-in appointments, either. If you'll tell me what this is regarding, I can direct you to the proper office."

She took a deep breath. "It's about a fugitive from the States."

The woman's brows rose. "By what name?"

"Isabel Sanborn."

She scribbled it on a sticky note. "Have you any identification?"

After a short hesitation, Isabel gave her the fake ID for Isabel Sanchez. The receptionist looked at it, and then back at her. Narrowing her eyes, she made a copy of the card and returned it to Isabel. "Have a seat and someone will be right with you."

Nodding, she walked toward the lacquered wood chairs, but remained standing. She was too nervous to sit still, and she'd been seated all night. Trying not to pace, she crossed her arms over her chest and focused on breathing. Although the building was air-conditioned, her cheeks felt hot and her palms were slick with perspiration.

"Miss Sanchez?"

She turned to face an older gentleman in a navy suit. He had a cup of coffee in one hand and a Danish in the other.

"I'm Officer Lutz," he said, lifting the pastry. "Right this way."

She came forward on shaky legs, preceding him into a small office. This time she took the seat she was offered.

He gave her a canny look. "I checked the database for Isabel Sanborn and saw her photo. I must say, the two of you bear a startling resemblance."

"The ID is fake," she admitted.

Lutz sat behind his desk and regarded her with relish, biting into the Danish. Without meaning to, she watched his movements hungrily. Her stomach was so empty it hurt. "Coffee?" he asked, taking a sip.

"No, thank you. I want to get this over with."

"By all means."

"I came here to turn myself in. I don't have any money and I need assistance in returning to the U.S. as soon as possible."

"How long have you been in Guatemala?"

"Two days."

"Where were you before that?"

She moistened her lips. "I'd rather not say."

Officer Lutz polished off the pastry and picked up a sheet of paper, scanning its contents. "I've been notified that you are a person of interest in two separate assaults in Mexico. A stabbing and a shooting."

She rubbed her forehead, starting to panic. This was

an unsettling complication. Maybe she should have stayed with Brandon.

He folded his hands on the surface of his desk, his gaze wandering over her slim form. "I have a hard time believing you accomplished these feats by yourself," he said, squinting. "Pretty little thing like you."

Isabel tried not to be insulted by his baiting chauvinism. She could hardly insist on her own guilt. "I'll talk about that as soon as I'm in American custody," she said, praying she wouldn't be extradited to Mexico.

"You're in an American embassy. Quite safe."

"I won't feel safe until I'm back in the U.S." Maybe not even then.

He made a harrumphing noise and shuffled the papers on his desk, as if preparing to leave the room.

"Please don't contact the Mexican government," she said, gripping the arms of her chair. Every nerve in her body was on high alert.

"Relax, Ms. Sanborn," he said, smiling wide enough to show his silver-capped molars. "My allegiance is to the U.S. only and I'm not influenced by outside entities. I also have the authority to make arrests, so I'd advise you to remain seated."

She loosened her grip on the chair, but she didn't relax. She couldn't trust this man. Memories of the recent assault bombarded her, making her feel powerless. The walls of the office closed in on her like a tomb.

Lutz's desk phone rang, startling her with its loud trill.

"Excuse me," he said, picking up the receiver. His eyes never left hers as he spoke in monosyllabic replies. After he ended the call, he rose from his chair, straightening his necktie. "I'll be right back. Are you sure you don't want coffee?"

She shook her head, mute.

The instant he was out of the door, she leaped to her feet. Heart racing, she grabbed a letter opener from the surface of his desk. A moment later Officer Lutz reappeared in the doorway, Brandon at his side. She stared at them with feral eyes, holding the impromptu weapon in a death grip.

Brandon's expression softened with sympathy and she realized how crazy she looked. Shoulders slumping, she set the letter opener down and returned to her seat. So much for maintaining her dignity.

Officer Lutz exchanged a puzzled glance with Brandon. "This is Deputy Marshal Knox. He says the two of you are already acquainted."

They were acquainted, all right. Intimately acquainted.

"He has a warrant for your arrest and a plane ticket with your name on it. Everything checks out."

"I won't go with him," she said, brimming with defiance.

"I'm sorry, Miss Sanborn. You don't have a choice."

She turned her gaze to Brandon, who appeared tired rather than triumphant. With his heavy beard stubble and mismatched clothes, he was an irresistible wreck. He must have tailed her here and allowed her to surrender, doing her one last kindness before he moved in for the kill. Or maybe he'd only been looking out for number one, avoiding a dramatic confrontation and flying fists.

She covered her face with a shaking hand, defeated and humiliated. If only she could crawl into a little ball and have a good cry. Instead she wiped away the tears and lifted her chin, pulling herself together.

"Can we get some breakfast?" he asked Lutz. "My detainee is obviously starving."

Chapter 16

Brandon read her the Miranda rights over breakfast.

The experience was surreal, but Isabel was too hungry to dwell on it. She cleaned her plate and pretended he wasn't there. The man she thought she knew didn't exist, and she hated Deputy Knox with a passion.

Before they left the embassy, a local doctor checked her ear, confirming a minor tear in the tympanic membrane. Air pressure couldn't harm an eardrum that had already been ruptured, so she was cleared to fly. Officer Lutz drove them to the airport, where they boarded a plane to Los Angeles within the hour.

The takeoff was unremarkable; the tension, unbearable.

"I'm sorry," he said finally, his face taut.

She ignored him.

"I shouldn't have touched you. It was wrong and I regret it."

His apology hurt, like hard fingers poking a bruise. She

wanted him to regret lying to her, not taking her to bed. "Are you going to tell your superior?"

"Yes."

"Will you get fired?"

"Probably."

The vindictive satisfaction she expected to feel didn't come. There was only a vague emptiness inside her, dark and quiet.

He swore under his breath. "I wish you'd just let me have it."

She frowned at him. "What?"

"Get mad at me," he said in a furious whisper. "I can't stand your silence!"

Her eyes widened in faux concern. "Oh, no! Are you uncomfortable? How terrible. Let's talk it out so you can feel at ease."

A muscle in his jaw flexed. "I don't give a damn about feeling at ease. I want to make things right between us."

"Nothing will ever be right between us."

He studied her mouth for a moment. "You begged me to make love to you."

She gritted her teeth, longing for a dagger to brandish. "Don't flatter yourself, Deputy Knox."

"Deputy Marshal Knox," he corrected. "But you can call me Brandon."

"I didn't beg *you* to make love to me. I begged someone else to make love to me. I don't even know you."

"Almost everything I told you about myself was true."

"Oh, really? Are you a self-defense expert who assesses risk for a living?"

"I teach self defense at the academy," he said, frowning. "And my last assignment involved risk management."

"Your last undercover assignment?"

He inclined his head.

Bastard. "You told me you'd planned this trip with your dead friend. I can't think of a more despicable lie."

His gaze darkened. "It wasn't a lie."

"And I suppose my article really inspired you?"

He flinched, rubbing a hand over his jaw. "It was a great article, Isabel."

"Oh, shut up. Everything you told me about yourself was designed to appeal to me on an intimate level. You knew exactly which angle to play."

"No. I was being real."

"You lied to me."

"Not about my family. Not about my feelings."

She glanced away, refusing to listen.

"Everything I said in that hotel room was true, Isabel."

Her throat went tight. "You used me."

"And you didn't use me?" he said, his voice hoarse with emotion. "You snuck out the door as soon as I fell asleep! Tell me that wasn't planned."

She shook her head, mute.

"Were you just saying what I wanted to hear in bed? Wearing me out so you could slip away?"

"Yes."

His mouth thinned with anger, though she doubted he believed her.

"Let's just forget it happened," she said.

"Not a chance. Even if you faked every orgasm, you're the best I've ever had."

She squeezed her eyes shut, holding the tears at bay. He knew she hadn't faked anything. "Damn you," she whispered, wishing she could hate him.

He stared out the window for a long time, pensive. "I don't think any charges will be brought against you for the incidents in Mexico. The stabbing was obviously done in self-defense and my reports will reflect that. I have to advise you to cooperate with the D.A.'s office and tell the truth about Jaime Carranza's death."

"Can I call my mother when we get to L.A.?"

"Of course," he said, his tone softening. "She's already been notified. You'll be able to speak to her as soon as we arrive."

Her stomach twisted with tension. She wasn't sure her mom would be happy to hear from her, after everything Isabel had put her through. "Carranza threatened to pay her a visit," she said, shuddering at the memory.

"When?"

She gave him an abbreviated version of what happened in the tomb before he arrived, describing the conference call from Carranza.

"He won't stop hunting you," Brandon said. "At some point you'll be asked to enter a Witness Protection Program. For your mother's safety as well as your own. If she doesn't know where you are, Carranza has no reason to go after her."

She raked a trembling hand through her hair. The news wasn't unexpected, but she was still devastated by the prospect of assuming another false persona. Which was worse, being locked up or continuing to live in exile?

"It's an excellent program," he said.

"Who runs it?"

"The U.S. Marshals Service."

Her lips parted in surprise. "Will you know where I am?"

"No. I don't work for that department. Even if I did, I wouldn't have access to your information unless I was assigned to protect you."

She nodded, feeling bleak. It wasn't easy to accept that she was never going to see anyone she loved again.

"Try to get some rest," he suggested. "You look exhausted."

Taking the pillow and blanket he offered, she turned her face away, hiding the tears that spilled down her cheeks.

Brandon watched Isabel sleep for few moments, struck by her beauty. He wished he could smooth the dark hair away from her brow and press his lips to her cool forehead. Draw her into his arms, kiss away the pain.

He glanced out at the snow-white clouds, squinting a little. His eyes felt grainy from lack of sleep, oversensitive to light. Shutting the window shade, he reclined his seat, needing the rest. But his mind wouldn't stop spinning.

He hadn't lied to Isabel—much. He'd loved her article. He missed his friend Jacob. And he'd meant every word he'd said in bed. Every hushed compliment, every hoarse whisper. He regretted the circumstances, not the sex.

He would probably get fired.

She shifted beside him, moaning in her sleep. Her face looked troubled, as if she was having a bad dream. He readjusted her pillow against his shoulder and put his arm around her, bringing her head to his chest. When she relaxed instantly, snuggling closer, a strong wave of protectiveness washed over him.

He didn't want to let her go.

Even if he kept his job, and requested a transfer to WITSEC, he couldn't choose his placement. He wouldn't be assigned to protect a woman with whom he'd had a personal relationship. And he couldn't go into hiding with her. Only spouses and children were allowed to enter the program with a witness.

Feeling numb, he stroked her slender arm. She murmured his name, her soft breath fanning his neck. Her dark hair was spilled over his shoulder, and the hem of her dress had ridden partway up, revealing her slender thighs.

Smothering a groan, he looked away. But he couldn't stop the barrage of sensual images. He'd done almost everything he could think of to her in that hotel room. He'd turned her on her belly and rained kisses on her lush little bottom. When that didn't seem like quite enough, he'd spanked her soft flesh, watching it turn pink. She'd squirmed and moaned and gotten deliciously wet, begging him to finish her.

He'd always had an active sex life, but he'd never been so insatiable, or so demanding. And she'd given as good as she got, driving him crazy with her hungry mouth.

He flushed at the memories, his erection swelling against his fly. After burying himself inside her a number of times yesterday, he should have been slow to react, and quick to settle. He wasn't.

The flight attendant passed by, preparing a lunch cart. They were in the back row of first class, which was typical for fugitive transport, and the flight was nowhere near capacity. Several empty rows stood between them and a handful of other passengers.

The extra privacy didn't help his condition.

Isabel stirred at the sound of drinks service, lifting her head. He gave her an even stare. She moved her sleepy gaze from his taut face to his distended fly. She straightened abruptly, pushing away from him.

Brandon lowered his lunch tray, heat creeping up his neck.

A flight attendant appeared beside him, offering cool refreshments. In addition to lemon-lime soda, she brought a bland lunch that he ate but barely tasted. The only notable item on the menu was a tangerine, and that was be-

cause he enjoyed watching Isabel fondle it. She peeled
the skin and ate it section by section, her eyes half-lidded.

"I have to pee," she announced after the trays were
cleared.

He rose at once, escorting her to the restroom at the
back of the plane. It was less than ten feet from their seats,
but he waited outside as per procedure. She flushed the
toilet and pushed open the sliding door a moment later.
Instead of stepping out, she looked down the aisle, as if
making sure no one was watching them.

They exchanged a heated glance.

Brandon couldn't have explained what happened next.
He'd apologized for touching her and knew better than to
do it again. She was his prisoner now, not just his target,
and so off-limits it wasn't even funny.

But his professional ethics, already in shreds, dissolved
under one come-hither gaze. When she grabbed the front
of his shirt and pulled him forward, he went eagerly, locking the door behind him.

She threaded her fingers through his hair and kissed
him, smashing her breasts to his chest, winding her tongue
around his. It was a sultry kiss, hot and impatient and a
little angry. When she bit his lower lip, harder than was
playful, he groaned and trapped her against the door, plundering her mouth.

She shoved at his chest, as if he was being too aggres-
sive. He released her at once, breaking contact. To his surprise, she drew back her arm and slapped him across the
face, hard. "This doesn't mean I forgive you."

He touched his stinging cheek. "What does it mean?"

Her eyes filled with tears. She wouldn't say.

Brandon didn't want to talk anyway. He crushed his
mouth over hers, ending the painful conversation. She
made an urgent sound and put her hands all over him,

gripping his shoulders and tugging at his shirt buttons. She tasted like citrus, tart and sweet. Desperate to have her, he raked her skirt up, palming her beautiful backside.

She tore her mouth from his and turned around, gathering the dress at her waist. Then she pushed her panties down her thighs, baring her bottom. "Hurry," she said, glancing over her shoulder at him. With limited space, and no flat surface to lift her up against, this was the only position they could manage.

Shaking with excitement, he fumbled with the zipper of his pants.

She braced herself against the door and bent forward slightly, standing on tiptoe to deal with their height differential. He gripped the base of his shaft and placed the tip against her, nudging her hot little sex. "I don't have a condom."

"It should be okay. Wrong time of month."

Taking a shocking risk, he entered her with one thrust, plunging into her. She gasped, holding on to the handrail to steady herself. He gritted his teeth at the heady sensation of being inside her with no barriers between them. She felt sleek, wet, tight, luscious. He wasn't going to last a minute.

Raising his hands to her breasts, he cupped her soft flesh, squeezing gently. Her nipples poked at the thin fabric of her dress, burning into the centers of his palms. Pushing aside the bodice, he pinched one taut peak, then the other. She shuddered with pleasure, her inner muscles clenching him like a silky fist.

Groaning, he kissed the side of her neck and smoothed his hand down her belly, feathering his fingertips between her legs. She was stretched open, her tender flesh exposed to his touch. He told her how sweet she felt, panting against her ear. "Wet my fingers," he said, lifting them to her mouth.

She licked his fingertips daintily. His erection throbbed inside her.

"More," he demanded.

Drawing two fingers inside her mouth, she sucked harder, getting him really wet.

"Good," he said, lowering his slick fingertips to her swollen cleft. He strummed her sweet spot, bringing her to the edge of orgasm. Then he backed off, raising his hand to her lips again. Moaning, she sucked his fingers and squirmed on his shaft, driving him crazy. He grasped her hips tightly, lifting her up and letting her slide back down on him.

They both groaned, wanting more.

"Please," she said, biting the end of his finger.

He stroked her needy sex again, circling her plump little nub. "Like this?" he asked, flicking his tongue over her earlobe.

She came apart in his arms, her hips bucking, body convulsing around him. Unable to hold back a moment longer, he withdrew a few inches and buried himself to the hilt. She sobbed his name, lost in the throes of orgasm. Loving the feel of her, loving *her,* he drove deep, thrusting hard enough to rattle the door. He knew he was using her too vigorously, but she wasn't complaining, and he couldn't stop.

He couldn't pull out, either.

Seconds before climaxing, he groaned, gripping her hips. "I'm going to come inside you."

"Yes," she panted.

Her permission didn't make it right, and her assertion that it was the wrong time of month didn't make it safe.

Disregarding the consequences, he slammed into her, driven by a primal urge to fill her any way he could.

With a muffled shout, he exploded, spilling himself deep inside her.

For several long seconds, he braced his hand against the door, half-collapsed, still connected to her. When he could breathe again, he moistened a couple of paper towels, handing them to her while he withdrew.

She straightened, holding the paper towels between her legs. He was too enthralled by the experience to regret his actions.

Almost.

She used the paper towels and set her clothes to rights. He tucked in and zipped up, his neck hot with shame. He'd never had unprotected sex before and he wasn't sure what to say. Apologizing didn't seem appropriate. Should he tell her he was clean?

Instead of discussing his health or sexual history, he framed her face with one hand, wanting to say something that really mattered. "I love you."

"Don't," she whispered, closing her eyes.

"Don't say it, or don't feel it?"

"Both. It hurts too much."

He didn't want to cause her any more pain, so he respected her request and fell silent. She avoided his gaze, maintaining an emotional distance that cut him to the bone. He'd touched her body, not her heart. There would be no soulful goodbyes.

Shrugging away from him, she slipped out the door.

They suffered the rest of the flight in silence.

Isabel had never felt more miserable. She couldn't deny her feelings any longer. Although she was mad at Brandon for lying to her, she was also desperately in love with him, and she dreaded their inevitable separation.

Why did she have to fall for him, of all people? Why now, at the worst possible moment in her life?

She hated this ending. A down-and-dirty quickie in a public restroom was the least romantic thing she could think of. It wasn't the bittersweet memory that would sustain her while she pined away for him in prison. Or Antarctica.

Brandon seemed as devastated by the situation as she was. She didn't know if she could trust what he'd told her in bed. In her experience, men said a lot of things they didn't mean. Then they left.

Out of sight, out of mind.

They gained time on the way to L.A., so somehow it was still sunny when they arrived. The longest day in the world. Jet-lagged and heartsick, she trudged through the airport with Brandon and two uniformed escorts. They informed her of her rights and handcuffed her in the back of the squad car.

Brandon's eyes flashed with annoyance, as if he didn't feel the measure was necessary, but he probably had no say in the matter. His mission, to deliver her into custody, was complete. He rode along as they drove her to the sheriff's department for questioning. They brought her in through a side entrance. Her mother was sitting in a chair in the hall.

Isabel's face crumpled at the sight.

Ana leaped to her feet, gathering Isabel into her arms. Isabel couldn't return the embrace because her wrists were secured behind her back. So she let her mother do all the hugging, but cried along with her.

"Who's this?" Ana asked when they broke apart, glancing at Brandon.

He shook her hand, introducing himself as Deputy Marshal Knox. "I brought your daughter into custody."

"Thank you," Ana said, hugging him, too. "Thank you for bringing her home safe."

Brandon patted her mom's shoulder, visibly uncomfortable. "You're welcome, ma'am. It's just my job."

Isabel's handcuffs were removed and she was led to a nearby interrogation room. Her mother waited outside but Brandon couldn't stay. He also had higher authorities to answer to. "Good luck," he said, holding her gaze.

She nodded, blinking back tears.

After a last look that would haunt her forever, he continued down the hall. Isabel sat at a small table, across from two detectives, a male and a female. For the next several hours, she gave a detailed account of Jaime's last night, her life on the run and her time with Brandon. The only lies she told were ones of omission. Their sexual encounters were no one's business, and she didn't *really* want him to get fired. He'd served her bravely and she was grateful, even if it was "just his job."

When she finished telling her story, the detectives left the room. Isabel sipped a drink from the vending machine and waited for them to return. After a short break, the female detective, Sergeant McAdams, came back without her partner.

"I have a couple of questions," she said, offering a hesitant smile.

Isabel shrugged. Other than an inappropriate relationship with Brandon, she had nothing to hide.

"Why did you leave Deputy Marshal Knox in the hotel room in San Marcos?"

"I'd planned to go to the embassy without him."

"Why?"

"Before I knew his real identity, I wanted to protect

him. I didn't see any reason for him to come forward with
me and risk being targeted by the drug cartel."

"How did you feel when you found out he was a U.S.
Marshal?"

"Betrayed," she said, taking a sip of soda. "I thought
he was my friend."

"Just a friend?"

"Yes."

"He didn't make any advances?"

"Never," she said truthfully. Isabel had made all of
those herself.

McAdams folded her hands on top of the table. "It's
not unusual for sexual assault victims to attempt to erase
the traumatic incident with a more pleasurable encounter.
They look for a safe partner. A friend, if you will."

Her stomach twisted with unease. "I wasn't assaulted."

"Attempted rape is assault."

"Oh," she said, feeling small.

"In all sexual assault cases we recommend a physical exam, from an E.R. doctor or your own gynecologist.
DNA swabs are taken."

"There's no evidence to collect."

"It's just procedure," McAdams assured her.

Isabel wasn't going to comply with a tissue swab, but
that was between her and the doctor she visited. "Am I
being charged with a crime?"

Sergeant McAdams leveled with her. "Not at this time.
Your statements match Deputy Marshal Knox's exactly,
with one notable exception. He admits to having inter-
course with you in the hotel room in San Marcos."

Her heart plummeted. Although he'd promised to be
honest, she hadn't expected him to be *this* honest.

"Was the encounter consensual?"

She hesitated, unsure how to respond.

"Did Deputy Marshal Knox rape you?"

"No!"

"Were you afraid of him?"

"No."

"Did he coerce or intimidate you?"

"Absolutely not," she said, her temper flaring. "He was a perfect gentleman. If anything, I coerced *him*. You can put that in your record."

McAdams leaned forward in her chair. "Complications like this muddy the legal waters and don't strengthen a case against the Carranza cartel. If you're willing to testify to the events you've described, refuse a DNA swab and sign a statement denying any unethical behavior by Deputy Marshal Knox, no charges will be brought against you."

"Not even for Jaime's death?"

"As long as you uphold your promise to testify against Carranza, we'll honor the deal and close that case."

"Done," Isabel said.

After she completed the paperwork, which took several hours, Isabel was allowed to see her mother again. They were visited by a man who worked for the Federal Witness Protection Program. He explained the relocation process while they listened, hand in hand.

"I'll go with you," her mother said.

"No way," Isabel protested. "What about the rest of the family? You'd never see them again." Her mother was happily remarried, and Isabel's stepdad had three teenage daughters. He would never leave them.

"You'll be able to write letters to your mother," the deputy marshal explained. "She can read them at a designated location, once per month, but she won't be able to keep copies, and the communication will be monitored."

"How can I contact her?" Ana asked.

"With letters, the same way. No phone calls, no emails, no social media."

Isabel watched her mother struggle with the concept, her face lined with worry. "How soon do I have to go?"

"Tomorrow or the next day. You'll stay in a safe room at the station until we place you. If your mother can pack a bag for you, with sensible clothes and shoes for any kind of weather, that would be very helpful."

Any kind of weather? Her heart sank. "I want to be near the ocean."

His smile was impersonal. "We'll see what we can do."

Isabel squeezed her mother's hand, trying to comfort her. This was better than jail. Better than death. And better than being on the run.

But it felt worse, somehow.

Chapter 17

Isabel slept for twelve hours straight.

When she woke the next morning, her mother returned with breakfast, an empty suitcase and an armful of garment bags. The safe room looked like a cheap studio apartment. There was a double bed, a small bathroom and a rickety wood-veneer table. After spending two years in similar places, Isabel felt right at home.

Her mother was a sight for sore eyes, too. She was still so pretty, with her petite figure and dark hair. If she colored it, Isabel couldn't tell. They talked about family, catching up on everything Isabel had missed while she was away. Her father's second wife had remarried; Isabel's stepsister was five.

Isabel told her mother a little of what had happened in Mexico, but she didn't want to upset her. Needing a distraction, she glanced at the piles of clothes. Although she'd showered last night and been given a pair of striped pajamas, she was eager to try on something new. "What did you bring me?"

Ana unzipped a garment bag, revealing about ten pairs of designer jeans. They looked vaguely familiar.

"You kept all of my clothes?"

"Of course," her mother said. "I have a closetful of your shoes, too. But I wasn't sure which ones to pack."

Isabel slipped off her pajama bottoms and rummaged through the jeans. Most of the styles were flashy, with faux rips and sparkly embellishments. She tried on the newest pair. They were too long to be worn with tennis shoes, and almost too tight to button. "I guess I've gained a few pounds."

"Yes. You were so skinny when you left."

Isabel heard the sadness in her mother's voice and felt sick with regret. "I'm sorry for putting you through that, Mama."

Ana squeezed her shoulder. "I'm just glad you're back, and healthy."

They found two pairs of older jeans that fit and rejected the rest. She also chose a few comfortable items—yoga pants and zippered sweatshirts, shorts and T-shirts, a few sundresses. Those, along with basic undergarments, went in the suitcase. The other stuff wasn't practical enough to pack. "Give it to Goodwill," Isabel said. "Or sell it to a consignment shop. This stuff must be worth thousands of dollars."

Shoes were her biggest extravagance, by far. Her mother had brought a variety of styles, from tall winter boots to flirty summer sandals. In Mexico, Isabel had longed for her expensive wardrobe and designer heels. Now that she had them back, she couldn't care less. Sighing, she selected three sensible pairs and tossed the others.

Her mother stared at her like she didn't recognize her.

"Thanks, Mom," she said, giving her a quick hug. "I'm sure I can buy anything else I need when I get there."

Ana wiped her eyes with a tissue, sniffling a little. "I wish I could go with you."

"I'll be fine."

She put on a brave smile. "Tell me about that marshal who rescued you."

Isabel's cheeks grew warm. Stalling for a moment, she finished dressing, pulling on a soft gray tracksuit.

"Was he nice?" Ana pressed.

She thought about their mile-high hookup. "Yes."

"Will he take you to your new home?"

"I don't think so," she said, shaking her head. Brandon might not have disclosed every detail of their affair, but he wouldn't be trusted to fly with her. "He doesn't work for the Witness Protection Program."

"Oh, that's too bad. I thought he liked you."

Isabel tried to stay strong, but all of her emotions were on edge. She sank into a chair at the table and covered her face with one hand.

"What's wrong?"

"I got attached to him," she whispered. "We…connected."

Ana looked as pleased as any mother who realized her daughter was infatuated with a man she approved of.

"But now I'm going away, and we'll never see each other again."

"He won't know where you are?"

"No."

Her mother pulled up a chair, hugging her close. Isabel couldn't hold in her tears. She cried in her mother's arms, feeling so defeated by circumstance. She wanted her family back, and she needed Brandon. Every day on the run, she'd longed for closeness and contentment. Peace seemed farther away than ever.

"I missed you so much," she said, her heart breaking. "I've spent the past two years regretting the hurt I caused you before I left. I'd do anything to make it up to you."

"Oh, honey," her mother said, smoothing her hair. "When I saw you yesterday, so beautiful and grown-up, all of my pain disappeared. I never blamed you for reacting badly to your father's death. I only wanted you to be safe."

She broke down completely, sobbing like a child who knew she was about to lose her mother for the second time.

Chapter 18

One month later.

Brandon spent the first half of the day surfing. He'd been at USMS headquarters for several weeks, wrapping up loose ends and doing an endless amount of paperwork. When a deputy marshal killed a man, he had to complete a mind-numbing round of medical tests and psychological evaluations.

Now he was back in San Diego, on leave.

He didn't know why he hadn't been fired. His actions in the hotel room with Isabel were grounds for dismissal, as was forgetting to check in and a number of other infractions. He hadn't mentioned the incident on the plane. It was the only detail he kept private. And he continued to think about their goodbye-sex, replaying the sequence of events over and over in his mind.

He was appalled by his failure to use protection. The

risk of conception was low but he couldn't dismiss it. He hated the idea of her facing the consequences of his negligence alone. How was she? *Where* was she? Did she miss him? Insomnia plagued him. Sometimes, very late at night, he wished for the unlikely to occur.

If fate intervened, and Isabel became pregnant, could they be together again?

At noon, he rode a crumbling wave to shore and came in. He secured his surfboard in the bed of his truck and towel-changed by the side of the road, pulling on a pair of worn jeans and a faded T-shirt. It was a sunny December afternoon, like any other.

He'd take Southern California weather over steamy jungle heat any day.

Climbing into the driver's seat, he drove to a quiet neighborhood in Hermosa Beach. Isabel's mother, Ana, had lived at this address with her second husband for the past few years. Brandon hadn't called first. He wouldn't have known what to say.

When he knocked on her front door, she opened it, her eyes widening with recognition. "Marshal Knox."

"Brandon," he corrected.

"Has something happened to Isabel?"

"Not that I know of," he said, raking a hand through his hair. "I haven't heard anything. We aren't in contact."

The concern on her face changed to confusion. "Would you like to come in?"

"Sure."

She offered him iced tea, which he accepted. It tasted like flowers and water, sort of vague and refreshing. The cottage-style bungalow was decorated with shells and knickknacks and boardwalk memorabilia.

"Isabel told me you were in the movies," he commented, seeing no indication of horror-film kitsch.

"That's right," she said, gesturing toward a small office. There was a poster on the wall that featured a curvy brunette running down the beach in a blood-spattered bikini, her face contorted into a scream. The treatment was sexy and gory and over-the-top.

"Wow," he said, taking a closer look. Then he felt weird for admiring a hot photo of Isabel's mother.

She laughed at his expression, as if she understood what he was thinking.

Trying not to flush, he glanced at another picture, of Isabel with her father. She was holding a surfing trophy, smiling brilliantly at the camera. He was wearing black leather pants at the beach, his rock-star hair windblown.

"I'd show you Isabel's room, but she never had one at this house."

He nodded, following Ana back to the kitchen. They sat down at a small table and he drank his tea, unsure how to proceed. "Have you heard from her?"

"Yes," Ana said, smiling. "She wrote me a long letter. They wouldn't let me keep a copy but it was upbeat, and very heartfelt." Her voice faltered at the last word. "I'm proud of the way she's handled this."

"She's okay, then? Not too lonely?"

Her eyes softened. "I think she's putting on a brave face."

"Did she say anything about me?"

"Not specifically. They monitor the letters, so she wouldn't include anything she considered a secret."

Brandon's chest ached with disappointment. He wanted her to be safe, but he was so miserable without her.

"She mentioned you before she left."

He perked up. "Really?"

"Yes. She said the two of you had bonded in Mexico.

I know she was upset about being relocated. She didn't want to be separated from you."

"I'm in love with her," he blurted.

Ana took a sip of iced tea, showing no surprise at his confession. "Two years ago, Isabel was spoiled, angry and out of control. I feared she would end up like her father. Or, even worse, end up with a man like her father."

He thought about the hardships Isabel had overcome before she'd turned her life around, and loved her all the more for it.

"Now my daughter is a lovely young woman, sensible and mature, everything a mother could ask for. I always hoped she would settle down with a good person. Someone strong and honorable, like you."

He rubbed a hand over his jaw, feeling powerless over the situation. There was nothing he wouldn't do for Isabel. He could quit his job and ask to be relocated along with her, but he doubted such an idiotic request would be granted. Even if she wanted him by her side, the government liked him right where he was.

"Sometimes I wish I hadn't caught her," he said, shaking his head. "And I have one regret that keeps me up at night."

"What's that?"

"The last time we were together, I didn't...take precautions."

Ana's dark brows lifted. "Hmm."

Brandon shifted in the chair, heat climbing up his neck. He'd never felt more awkward, or less honorable.

"In her letter, Isabel made an offhand remark about having her period. I wasn't sure why she'd include that particular detail until now."

"Maybe she figured I'd stop by and talk to you," he said, frowning inwardly. He should have felt relieved by the news. An unwanted pregnancy would have been a disaster, not a blessing in disguise. "Thank you for telling me."

"Would you like me to relay a message to her?"

"No," he said, rising to his feet. "For her safety, I have to leave her alone. Now that I know she isn't...that we aren't...connected by anything, I can move on." The lie was so ridiculous, he almost choked on it. He would be connected to Isabel forever, and he had no interest in moving on.

"I'm sorry," Ana said kindly.

Brandon thanked her for her time and muttered a terse goodbye, walking out before his emotions could betray him.

Isabel didn't hate her new life.

Much.

It was bitterly cold in Kansas City. She resented the fact that she'd been placed as far away from the ocean as was possible in the continental U.S., but she'd quickly adjusted to the winter wonderland. She worked in a pizza joint, next to a wood-fired grill, so that helped. Over the past month she'd moved up in the ranks at the busy restaurant, going from washing dishes to making pies to waiting on customers.

The hard work didn't bother her; she enjoyed it. The other employees didn't bother her, either, although most of them were young men. With her pageboy haircut and baggy sweatshirts, she attracted almost no male attention. A woman had hit on her, in fact. She'd felt a little embarrassed but tried to take it in stride.

The worst part of her job, now that she'd moved to the front of the house, was seeing so many happy families. Casey's Pizza Company catered to teens and young couples with children. Every night of the week, kids were running up and down the aisles, playing video games and spilling drinks. There was always a baby crying somewhere. Always.

It was difficult to leave at the end of her shift, walking home in the snow alone, Christmas lights all around.

Her apartment wasn't nice but she liked it. She took pride in her chipped tile countertops and threadbare carpet. With her last paycheck, she'd bought a live pine tree and carried it up three flights of stairs, all by herself. Humming holiday songs, she'd decorated the branches with a sparkly silver garland and colorful strings of beads.

She'd also taken up running. Running wasn't as much fun as surfing, and downtown Kansas City was no tropical paradise. But she pounded the pavement so hard and often that she'd lost two pounds, despite her considerable pizza intake.

When she wasn't running, she was writing. Or reading. She'd missed having entire libraries of books at her disposal. Enrolling in junior college seemed like a reasonable option. With no family or friends to speak of, she had plenty of unfilled hours in the day.

At closing time, she left Casey's and pulled her hood over her head, trudging toward her lonely apartment. Snow flurries floated down from the dark sky, melting as soon as they landed. Grayish sludge squished beneath her boots and her breath puffed out in a little cloud of steam with every other step.

There was a letter in her mailbox!

Unlike her mother, Isabel was allowed to keep their correspondence. She had another letter, tucked under her pillow, that she read every night. This one was a Christmas card. She raced up the stairs, flying into her apartment and locking the door behind her.

After turning on the lamp in the living room, she hung up her coat and sat down with the card, opening it carefully.

Her mother gave an update on Dave and the rest of the family, making a vague allusion to their holiday plans. Isabel couldn't be a part of the festivities, so Ana didn't dwell on the details. She did say she missed Isabel terribly. The simple words brought tears to her eyes.

At the end of the note, her mother's tone changed from cheerful to cautious. Isabel read the last part three times, struggling to make sense of it:

I hope the following news doesn't upset you. An old friend visited, inquiring about your health. I couldn't give out any information, of course. It broke my heart to send him away empty-handed. He was very despondent.

After he left, I started worrying about the tiniest details. Are you taking care of yourself, getting enough rest? Please see a doctor about your menstrual cramps and let me know the results.

Love always,
Mom

It dawned on Isabel that her mother was asking about her period for a reason. She'd only mentioned it in the last letter to put inquiring minds at ease. The deputy marshal who monitored her correspondence knew about her affair with Brandon. Perhaps the odd remark had planted the seed of doubt in her mother's head.

Or maybe the "old friend" who'd visited was Brandon. Had he asked about her? Had he told her mother they'd had unprotected sex?

How *embarrassing*.

Cheeks flaming, she folded the letter and put it back inside the envelope. She didn't need to see a doctor about cramps. She'd had two regular periods since arriving in Kansas and she definitely wasn't pregnant.

For the next hour, she paced the living room, her thoughts racing. If Brandon had tracked down her mother, and come by in person to ask about her, he still cared. He was "very despondent."

She hadn't wanted to believe him when he said he loved her. She hadn't wanted to love him back, either. In the hotel room, she'd been wrapped up in the moment, high on pleasure. She'd loved everything about his performance in bed. She'd loved the way he touched her, the way he made her feel.

After their mile-high bathroom break, which was hot and needy and unromantic, she finally realized she was in love with *him*.

She hadn't been convinced that he returned the sentiment. Until now.

Curling up on the couch, she wrapped her arms around her body, which ached with emptiness.

After a long session of feeling sorry for herself, she leaped to her feet. Flipping open her cell phone, she called Deputy Marshal Shannon Peters, the woman who'd been assigned to protect her.

"I want out of the program," she said without preamble.

"It's totally normal to have difficulty adjusting in the first few months, Isabel. Tell me how you're feeling."

She gritted her teeth. "I don't want to do this anymore."

"You'd rather risk your mother's life?"

"I'd rather risk *my* life. I'd rather live! This isn't living."

"Give it a chance."

"Let me be a decoy," she said in a rush, inspired. "Dangle me in front of Carranza and I'll help you bring him in."

Shannon's laughter was like tinkling bells. "I'm sorry, Isabel. You're a civilian. It can't be done."

"Then deputize me. That can be done. According to my research, the U.S. Marshals are the only law enforcement team that holds the capability."

She clucked her tongue. "It's an archaic tactic from the Old West, rarely used nowadays. We don't endanger witnesses—we protect them. If you'd like to become a deputy marshal, you'll have to do it the hard way. Go to college and apply to the academy."

Isabel didn't want to be a marshal. She just wanted to be free.

"Can you hang in there for now? I might have some good news for you soon."

"What good news?"

Shannon's voice lowered to a conspiratorial whisper. "Manuel Carranza was involved in a shoot-out in downtown Tijuana a few days ago. According to reports, he's been seriously injured. Perhaps fatally."

Isabel's heart leaped. "If he dies, can I go home?"

"We would definitely reassess your situation."

They spoke for a few more moments before hanging up, and Isabel promised not to break her cover. For the time being, she was still Isabella Saunders, boyish pizza waitress from Rancho Mirage, California.

But as she stood by her glitzy tree and looked out the window, watching snowflakes drift down on the gleaming street, she felt like herself again.

Chapter 19

Isabel watched Brandon wade out of the cool blue Pacific, wet suit clinging to his lean body, surfboard tucked under one arm.

She waited by his truck, basking in the warm San Diego sun. Mid-seventies felt like heaven to her after a long December in Kansas City. Her heart raced in anticipation of seeing him again. After arriving this morning, she'd been told which beach he frequented and what type of vehicle he drove.

He didn't know she was coming. Brandon's boss was aware of his feelings for Isabel and agreed to keep the surprise.

The surf was high and the form looked fantastic. She'd never been to Sunset Cliffs before and she was eager to dive in. The desire to suit up and paddle out was strong, but not as strong as her need for Brandon.

When he spotted her, he stopped dead in his tracks.

Giggling with excitement, she waved both arms over her head. He tossed his surfboard on the ice plant along the path and started running, closing the distance between them in a pulse-pounding minute.

His hair had grown out a little, but the dye hadn't faded much. The effect was oddly adorable, dark with light roots.

She worried about her own cropped hair as his hungry gaze swept over her, taking in her slim-fitting jeans and snug tank top. She'd worn her most flattering outfit and even put on a bit of makeup. Now she felt paralyzed by self-consciousness.

He cupped her chin with one hand, as if he needed to touch her to make sure she wasn't a figment of his imagination. "Is it really you?"

She nodded, nibbling her lower lip.

"How did you get here?"

"By plane."

"To this beach, I mean."

"I took a taxi from the airport."

He glanced in the bed of his truck, where her suitcase was sitting. "Did you leave the program?"

"Sort of. I'm supposed to lie low for a while. Carranza died last night."

"I heard he was in critical condition."

"Right now they're evaluating my case, assessing any lingering threats. The man I stabbed made a full recovery, but he's locked up in Mexico on unrelated charges. The agency is 'monitoring the situation' and my release is conditional."

"On what?"

"I can't resume my identity as Isabel Sanborn or visit L.A. And I have to stay with an armed deputy for a few weeks."

"Who?"

She pointed at the center of his chest.

"Me? They released you to my protection?"

Heart racing, she twined her arms around his neck. "How do you feel about having a roommate?"

He just stared at her, speechless.

"I won't be any trouble," she promised, studying his face. "I thought I'd sign up for some online college classes. All I need is a computer, a surfboard and you."

His eyes darkened. "You need me?"

She did him one better. "I love you."

He backed her up against the passenger door and angled his mouth over hers, giving her the kind of kiss she'd spent two months dreaming about. Hot, demanding, breathless. Her hands slipped over his neoprene wet suit, finding no purchase.

"I love you, too," he said, breaking the kiss. "So much I didn't feel alive without you. Every night, I stayed awake, aching for you. Wondering if you were safe. I couldn't stand not knowing where you were."

Her chest tightened with emotion. "I was in Kansas City."

He swore under his breath.

She laughed, resting her forehead on his shoulder. "It wasn't that bad. I took up running. But the nights…were exactly what you described."

With a low groan, he bent his head again, brushing his lips over hers. Tasting her, filling her mouth with his tongue. The last kiss was an expression of their torturous time apart. This one was a promise of future pleasure.

"You're getting me wet," she said, shivering as salt water soaked into her tank top.

He ran back to retrieve his surfboard and secured it in

the bed of the truck, ushering her into the passenger seat. "Do you want to see your mom first?"

"I want to go to your place."

Grinning, he took off his wet suit on the side of the road, keeping a towel around his waist while he tugged on a pair of worn blue jeans and a gray T-shirt. California surfing had its perks. She'd never get tired of watching Brandon change.

"I like your hair, by the way," he said as he climbed into the driver's seat.

She smoothed a hand over her head. "Do you?"

"Yeah. It looks sexy."

Her entire body tingled with warmth. "Thanks. I like yours, too."

He made a skeptical sound and put the truck into gear, glancing in his rearview mirror. "What are you talking about? My hair looks like crap."

She smiled, finding him impossibly attractive. "Why'd you keep the color?"

"Because it reminded me of you."

Tears sprang into her eyes, but they were from a happy place. A well of joy. "I hope I'm not imposing too much by asking to live with you," she said, twisting her hands in her lap. "It's just temporary."

"Don't be ridiculous. You can stay as long as you want to. Forever, preferably."

She looked out at the majestic blue waves, her heart swelling with love for him. At one time, a statement like that would have made her feel closed in. Hearing it now opened up a whole new world. "You might reconsider after I wear out my welcome. Maybe you'll hate the sounds I make in my sleep."

"I love the sounds you make in your sleep."

"You could get annoyed by the way I brush my teeth."

"Do you do it naked?"

"No."

"That will be a problem then."

He pulled up to an upscale apartment complex a few miles from the beach. She remained seated, feeling anxious despite his relaxed attitude and easy jokes. "Will you have to go on an assignment soon?"

"I'm on mandatory leave for the next month, so I won't be going anywhere. They always give you time off when you kill someone."

Sympathy coursed through her, along with a healthy dose of guilt. She'd attended counseling in Kansas City and the nightmares weren't as frequent now. Her ear had also healed well and she'd regained a full range of hearing. "Had you done that before?"

"No. I don't care to repeat the experience, either. But I will if I have to. Sometimes I get dangerous assignments."

She fell silent for a moment, contemplative. He was warning her that living with him wouldn't always be easy. There was a drive inside him, pushing him to take risks. But she understood and accepted that tendency, because it was in her nature, too. "Sometimes I surf in dangerous conditions."

"I've noticed," he said wryly, turning off the engine. He left the driver's seat and walked around to open the passenger door for her. "As long as you come in when it gets too rough, I can handle that."

"Will you do the same?" she asked, meeting his sincere blue eyes.

"Yes. I promise."

Taking a deep breath, she accepted his hand and his word. Leaving his surfboard in the back of the truck, he grabbed her suitcase and they ascended the steps to his second-floor apartment. Her new home.

"What do you think?" he asked, arching a brow.

It was clean, modern, spacious. A little too spare and masculine for her tastes, but she could work with that. "Nice," she said, smiling.

He cleared his throat, appearing uncertain. "We don't have to...rush anything. If you want to order some take-out and watch movies, that sounds great to me."

"Me, too," she said, brushing past him. "Where's the bedroom?"

He gestured down the hall, his gaze darkening as she pulled her tank top over her head, letting it fall on the carpet. In the doorway, she paused, stripping off her jeans. He had a big, comfortable-looking bed and a gorgeous ocean view. Tummy fluttering with anticipation, she crawled across the mattress in her underwear. Here, with him, she felt safe, and loved, and free. "It's perfect," she said, opening her arms.

A second later, he joined her, and it *was* perfect. In every way.

* * * * *

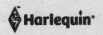

REQUEST YOUR FREE BOOKS!
2 FREE NOVELS PLUS 2 FREE GIFTS!

ROMANTIC
SUSPENSE

Sparked by Danger, Fueled by Passion.

YES! Please send me 2 FREE Harlequin® Romantic Suspense novels and my 2 FREE gifts (gifts are worth about $10). After receiving them, if I don't wish to receive any more books, I can return the shipping statement marked "cancel." If I don't cancel, I will receive 4 brand-new novels every month and be billed just $4.49 per book in the U.S. or $5.24 per book in Canada. That's a saving of at least 14% off the cover price! It's quite a bargain! Shipping and handling is just 50¢ per book in the U.S. and 75¢ per book in Canada.* I understand that accepting the 2 free books and gifts places me under no obligation to buy anything. I can always return a shipment and cancel at any time. Even if I never buy another book, the two free books and gifts are mine to keep forever.

240/340 HDN FEFR

Name _____ (PLEASE PRINT)

Address _____ Apt. #

City _____ State/Prov. _____ Zip/Postal Code

Signature (if under 18, a parent or guardian must sign)

Mail to the Reader Service:
IN U.S.A.: P.O. Box 1867, Buffalo, NY 14240-1867
IN CANADA: P.O. Box 609, Fort Erie, Ontario L2A 5X3

Not valid for current subscribers to Harlequin Romantic Suspense books.

Want to try two free books from another line?
Call 1-800-873-8635 or visit www.ReaderService.com.

* Terms and prices subject to change without notice. Prices do not include applicable taxes. Sales tax applicable in N.Y. Canadian residents will be charged applicable taxes. Offer not valid in Quebec. This offer is limited to one order per household. All orders subject to credit approval. Credit or debit balances in a customer's account(s) may be offset by any other outstanding balance owed by or to the customer. Please allow 4 to 6 weeks for delivery. Offer available while quantities last.

Your Privacy—The Reader Service is committed to protecting your privacy. Our Privacy Policy is available online at www.ReaderService.com or upon request from the Reader Service.

We make a portion of our mailing list available to reputable third parties that offer products we believe may interest you. If you prefer that we not exchange your name with third parties, or if you wish to clarify or modify your communication preferences, please visit us at www.ReaderService.com/consumerschoice or write to us at Reader Service Preference Service, P.O. Box 9062, Buffalo, NY 14269. Include your complete name and address.

HRS11B

Harlequin® Special Edition® is thrilled to present a new installment in USA TODAY *bestselling author RaeAnne Thayne's reader-favorite miniseries,* THE COWBOYS OF COLD CREEK.

Join the excitement as we meet the Bowmans—four siblings who lost their parents but keep family ties alive in Pine Gulch. First up is Trace. Only two things get under this rugged lawman's skin: beautiful women and secrets. And in Rebecca Parsons, he finds both!

Read on for a sneak peek of CHRISTMAS IN COLD CREEK. *Available November 2011 from Harlequin® Special Edition®.*

On impulse, he unfolded himself from the bar stool. "Need a hand?"

"Thank you! I…" She lifted her gaze from the floor to his jeans and then raised her eyes. When she identified him her hazel eyes turned from grateful to unfriendly and cold, as if he'd somehow thrown the broken glasses at her head.

He also thought he saw a glimmer of panic in those interesting depths, which instantly stirred his curiosity like cream swirling through coffee.

"I've got it, Officer. Thank you." Her voice was several degrees colder than the whirl of sleet outside the windows.

Despite her protests, he knelt down beside her and began to pick up shards of broken glass. "No problem. Those trays can be slippery."

This close, he picked up the scent of her, something fresh and flowery that made him think of a mountain meadow on a July afternoon. She had a soft, lush mouth and for one brief, insane moment, he wanted to push aside that stray lock of hair slipping from her ponytail and taste her. Apparently he needed to spend a lot less time working and a great deal *more* time recreating with the opposite sex if he could have sudden random fantasies about a woman he wasn't even inclined to like, pretty or not.

"I'm Trace Bowman. You must be new in town."

She didn't answer immediately and he could almost see the wheels turning in her head. Why the hesitancy? And why that little hint of unease he could see clouding the edge of her gaze? His presence was obviously making her uncomfortable and Trace couldn't help wondering why.

"Yes. We've been here a few weeks."

"Well, I'm just up the road about four lots, in the white house with the cedar shake roof, if you or your daughter need anything." He smiled at her as he picked up the last shard of glass and set it on her tray.

Definitely a story there, he thought as she hurried away. He just might need to dig a little into her background to find out why someone with fine clothes and nice jewelry, and who so obviously didn't have experience as a waitress, would be here slinging hash at The Gulch. Was she running away from someone? A bad marriage?

So…Rebecca Parsons. Not Becky. An intriguing woman. It had been a long time since one of those had crossed his path here in Pine Gulch.

Trace won't rest until he finds out Rebecca's secret, but will he still have that same attraction to her once he does?
Find out in CHRISTMAS IN COLD CREEK.
Available November 2011 from Harlequin® Special Edition®.

Harlequin®

ROMANTIC
SUSPENSE

CARLA CASSIDY

Cowboy's Triplet Trouble

Jake Johnson, the eldest of his triplet brothers, is stunned
when Grace Sinclair turns up on his family's ranch declaring
Jake's younger and irresponsible brother as the father of her
triplets. When Grace's life is threatened, Jake finds himself
fighting a powerful attraction and a need to protect. But as
the threats hit closer to home, Jake begins to wonder
if someone on the ranch is out to kill Grace....

A brand-new Top Secret Deliveries story!

Available in November wherever books are sold!

HRS27751